"I remember a time...

...when Jedi were not...

...generals but peacekeepers."

CONTENTS

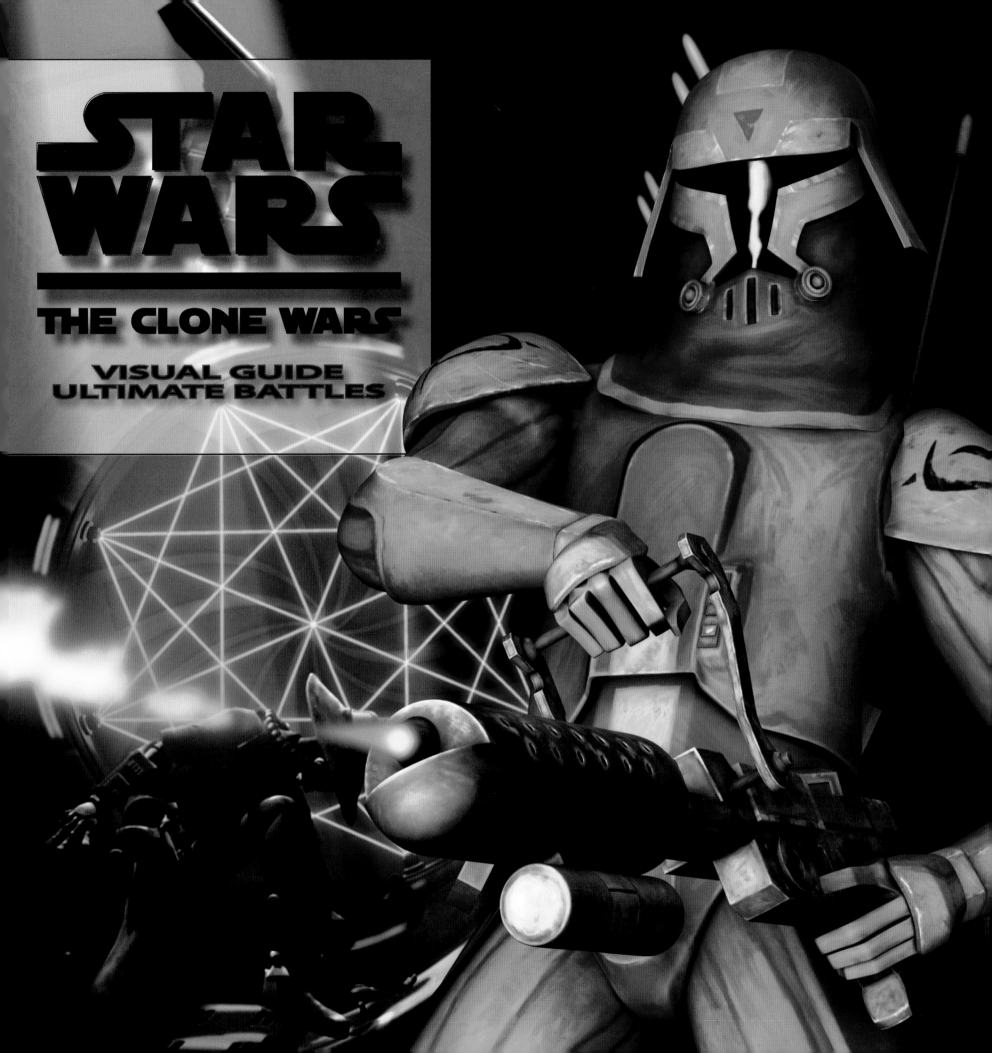

GALAXY OF PERIL

Across the galaxy, once-fair worlds are wreathed in smoke from the fires of war; their soil now tilled by the marching metal feet of Separatist battle droids and the boots of clone troopers born to die in service to the embattled Republic.

Stretched to a breaking point, the Jedi Knights struggle to tell friend from foe. They cling to their duty as keepers of the peace, even as they lead men into battle. But amid the nightmare of war, peace is but a dream.

Where order breaks down, pirates, bounty hunters, and mercenaries rush in, seeking to fill their coffers amid the chaos. And ancient enemies emerge from their hiding places, sensing a chance to settle old scores.

JEDI AT WAR

THE SEPARATIST THREAT has convinced the Jedi to abandon their traditional role as peacekeepers and now they serve Chancellor Palpatine as generals leading the Republic's clone armies. The Jedi Council sees this wartime bargain as necessary to save the galaxy, but it fears that the Order may lose its way in the conflict.

Close Combat

On Geonosis, the Jedi generals and the clone troops under their command fight side by side against the Separatists' hordes of battle droids.

Ahsoka Tano

A young Togruta, Ahsoka Tano is Anakin's Padawan. Like Anakin, she is passionate and rebellious.

Fighting for the Republic, the Jedi Knights must battle not just Separatists, but also deadly bounty hunters such as notorious mercenary Cad Bane.

Letting Go

Master Yoda assigns Ahsoka Tano to Anakin in hopes that letting go of a Padawan once she's ready to be a Jedi Knight will teach Anakin to let go of more dangerous attachments, too. The two are headstrong and argue often; both have much to learn. But a strong bond develops between them.

Obi-Wan Kenobi

Obi-Wan Kenobi is known for his skills as a diplomat. He is realistic and wise beyond his years.

Anakin Skywalker

Prophecy says Anakin Skywalker is the Chosen One who will bring balance to the Force.

Divided Loyalties

Anakin begins to struggle with his duty to the Jedi Order, the demands of being a general in the Republic military, the need to train Ahsoka Tano as a Jedi, and his secret marriage to Senator Padmé Amidala. Seeking help, Anakin increasingly turns to Chancellor Palpatine for his guidance and friendship.

YEARS OF
HUNTING HAVE
MADE HER
STRONG

RULE OF THE GUN

Even a law-abiding bounty hunter always makes sure to have a blaster close at hand: People with bounties on their heads are desperate and will do almost anything to avoid being brought back to whatever situation they've tried so hard to escape.

AURRA SING'S
HEAD HOUSES A
BIOCOMPUTER AND
ANTENNAE

TOPKNOT KEEPS
SUGI'S HAIR OUT
OF THE WAY

BLASTER IS
ALWAYS AT
THE READY

ODD JOBS

Hunting fugitives isn't the only way for a hired gun to earn money. When times are tough bounty hunters may work as mercenaries. The Zabrak Sugi and her crew agree to protect a Felucian village against a pirate gang.

UTILITY
POUCH

BOSSK'S FRILL STANDS UP WHEN HE'S ANGRY

COLLAR OF FLIGHT SUIT

BOUNTY HUNTERS

IN A WAR-TORN GALAXY, there are many places where police fear to go. That job often falls to bounty hunters—guns-for-hire who stalk wanted criminals and return them dead or alive. Some hunters are brave investigators who respect the law, but others are ruthless gunslingers who care only about money.

LAW OF THE HUNT

Whoever hires the hunter sets the rules and decides whether a fugitive is to be returned alive or dead. Law-enforcement authorities usually want fugitives to stand trial for their crimes, though they make exceptions for very dangerous criminals. Bounties can bring in just a few credits, or be worth millions to a hunter.

ALTERING THE DEAL

Sometimes hunters get in too deep and decide it's best to pass up a potential bounty when a job gets too dangerous. Klatooinian bounty hunter Castas regrets agreeing to work for Aurra Sing after she, Bossk, and Boba Fett destroy a Republic warship.

BIG GAME HUNTER

Bane has a formidable reputation in the underworld, where he's known as the greatest bounty hunter since Jango Fett lost his head.

CAD BANE

ONE OF THE GALAXY'S most dangerous bounty hunters, Cad Bane will work for anyone willing to pay his fee without worrying about what's right. Kidnapping, theft, and even murder are all just jobs to him. Bane will join forces with other hunters if he must, but he trusts no one and works alone whenever he can.

CUSTOMIZED PERSUADER PISTOL

GAUNTLETS HIDE TOOLS AND WEAPONS

SENSOR SUITE WITHIN CRANIUM

PRIMARY POWER UNIT

TODO 360

★ Todo 360 is a top-of-the-line techno-service droid built by Vertseth Automata, not a butler. But there are worse things than taking orders from a grumpy Cad Bane: You could find that you've been wired with powerful explosives.

HOME TURF

Not being Force-sensitive, Bane seeks to even the odds against the Jedi by using his surroundings as weapons. At Devaron, he counters Anakin Skywalker and his troops by controlling his ship's functions from his wrist-com. At Black Stall Station, he escapes by maneuvering Obi-Wan Kenobi and Mace Windu into a grid of deadly laser beams.

MITRINOMON JETPACK THRUSTER

DURASTEEL MAGNO-GRIP BOOTS

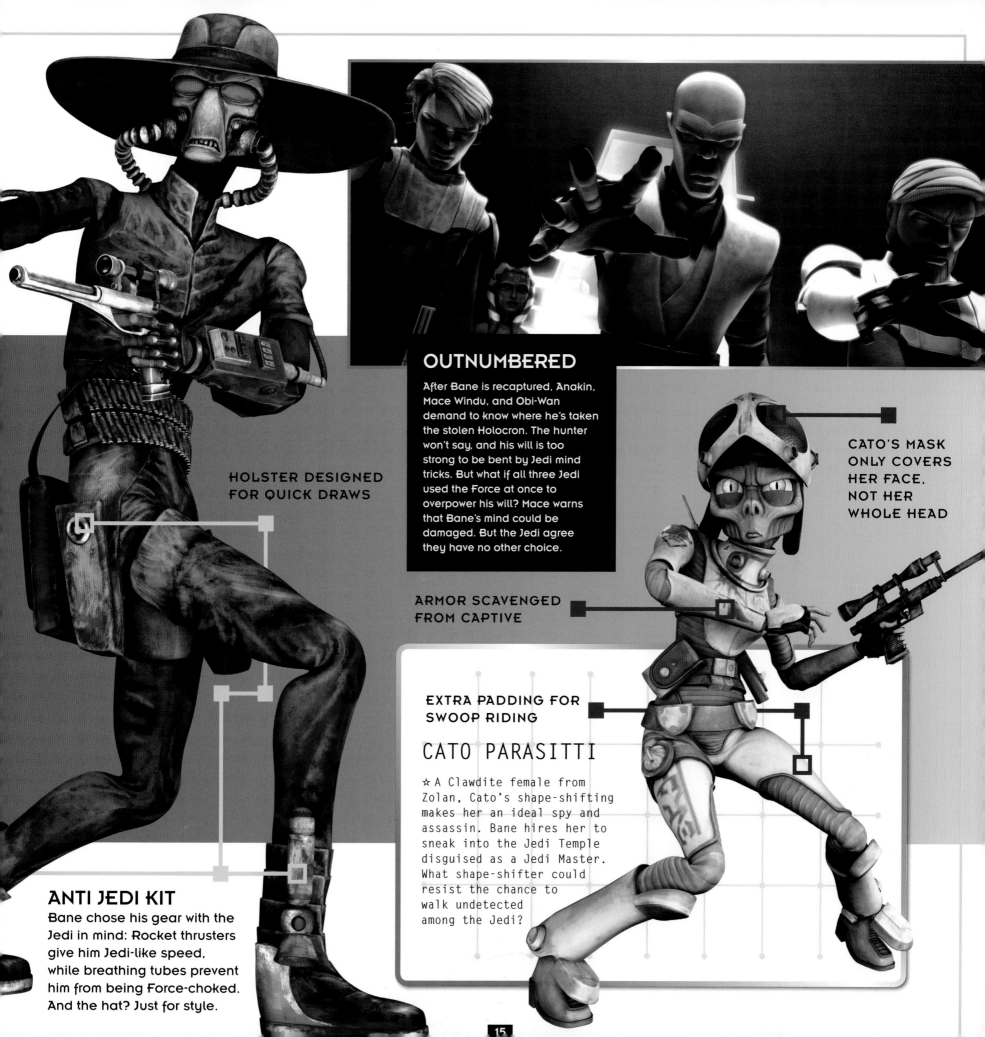

OUTNUMBERED

After Bane is recaptured, Anakin, Mace Windu, and Obi-Wan demand to know where he's taken the stolen Holocron. The hunter won't say, and his will is too strong to be bent by Jedi mind tricks. But what if all three Jedi used the Force at once to overpower his will? Mace warns that Bane's mind could be damaged. But the Jedi agree they have no other choice.

HOLSTER DESIGNED FOR QUICK DRAWS

CATO'S MASK ONLY COVERS HER FACE, NOT HER WHOLE HEAD

ARMOR SCAVENGED FROM CAPTIVE

EXTRA PADDING FOR SWOOP RIDING

CATO PARASITTI

★ A Clawdite female from Zolan, Cato's shape-shifting makes her an ideal spy and assassin. Bane hires her to sneak into the Jedi Temple disguised as a Jedi Master. What shape-shifter could resist the chance to walk undetected among the Jedi?

ANTI JEDI KIT

Bane chose his gear with the Jedi in mind: Rocket thrusters give him Jedi-like speed, while breathing tubes prevent him from being Force-choked. And the hat? Just for style.

VILLAIN IN DISGUISE

After escaping Cad Bane's ship, Captain Rex's clone troopers remove their helmets to await a meal and a well-earned rest. But Ahsoka worries about one clone who shuffles off clutching an injured arm.

1 As Ahsoka tries to be of help, Anakin sees something suspicious: The injured trooper is leaking green blood. It's Cad Bane in disguise!

"YOU'RE NO CLONE!"

2 Bane knees Ahsoka in the stomach and races for a V-19 starfighter, rocketing away from the *Resolute* before Anakin can stop him.

3 As Bane's starfighter disappears, Anakin realizes the bounty hunter still has the names of countless Jedi children. The Council must be told!

MASTER OF THE SENATE

As Naboo's Senator, Palpatine made life difficult for his own Chancellor, so he's not surprised by the burdens of his office. Senators have many different interests: some want peace at any cost, while others hunger for war. Palpatine must use promises, persuasion, guile, and the occasional harsh word to keep the Republic following his plan.

CHANCELLOR
PALPATINE

THE LEADER OF the Republic, Chancellor Palpatine has reluctantly served extra terms in office and taken up emergency powers to direct the galaxywide war against the Separatists. His duties include working with the Senate to fund the war, discussing military strategy with the Jedi, negotiating with the megacorporations, and trying to reassure the galaxy's worried people that peace will return.

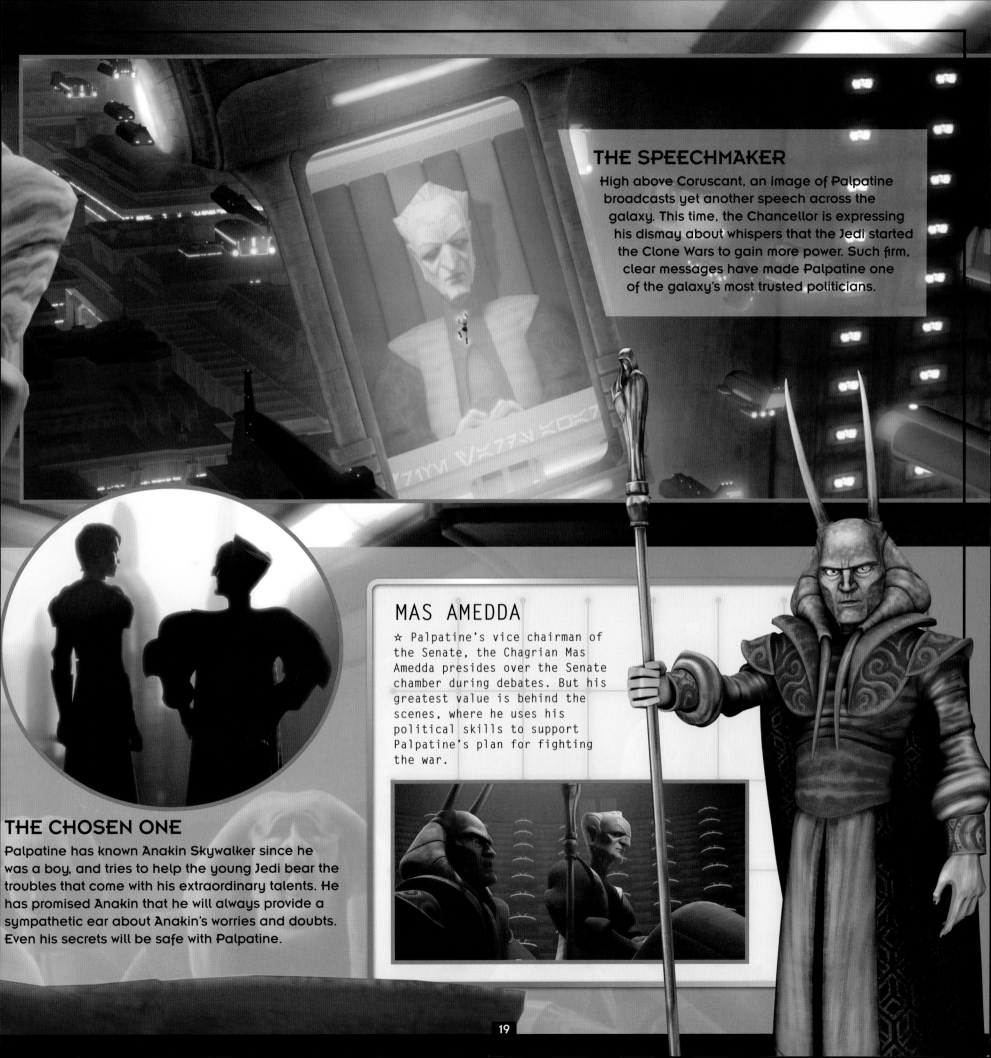

THE SPEECHMAKER

High above Coruscant, an image of Palpatine broadcasts yet another speech across the galaxy. This time, the Chancellor is expressing his dismay about whispers that the Jedi started the Clone Wars to gain more power. Such firm, clear messages have made Palpatine one of the galaxy's most trusted politicians.

MAS AMEDDA

☆ Palpatine's vice chairman of the Senate, the Chagrian Mas Amedda presides over the Senate chamber during debates. But his greatest value is behind the scenes, where he uses his political skills to support Palpatine's plan for fighting the war.

THE CHOSEN ONE

Palpatine has known Anakin Skywalker since he was a boy, and tries to help the young Jedi bear the troubles that come with his extraordinary talents. He has promised Anakin that he will always provide a sympathetic ear about Anakin's worries and doubts. Even his secrets will be safe with Palpatine.

COUNCIL OF WAR

THE JEDI COUNCIL CONSISTS of twelve Jedi selected for their wisdom and years of experience. Led by Yoda, the Council meets in a chamber atop one of the five towers of Coruscant's Jedi Temple. There, the Jedi discuss the business of the Order, plan war against the Separatists, and try to determine the will of the Force.

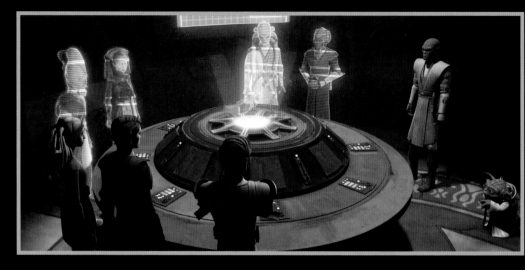

DISTANT VOICES

With many Jedi serving as generals in the Republic military, it is now rare for all twelve members of the Jedi Council to be on Coruscant at the same time. Council members who are offworld attend meetings by hologram, which enables them to see and hear their colleagues as if they were together.

MACE WINDU

A battle-hardened Jedi, Mace is determined to defeat the Separatists, but thinks little of the Republic's political leaders, dismissing most as either corrupt or weak. Mace is second only to Yoda within the ranks of the Order.

YODA

The Grand Master of the Order, Yoda has trained countless Younglings and Padawans in his centuries of service to the galaxy, and has advised many leaders of the Republic. But he fears dark days are near for the galaxy and its Jedi.

ADI GALLIA

Adi Gallia is respected as a warrior and a diplomat. Adi was close to Qui-Gon Jinn and sees a lot of Jinn in Anakin.

The Jedi have kept the peace in the Republic for thousands of years, but now those who guide the Order wonder how to help the galaxy survive the clone wars.

EETH KOTH

Eeth Koth has seen the evils of the Separatists firsthand on worlds such as Geonosis, where he barely survived the initial battle of the war. His skill with a lightsaber and ability to endure pain make him a formidable opponent.

KIT FISTO

A Nautolan Jedi known for his ready smile, Kit Fisto is beloved by the Temple's younglings. But beneath his grin, Kit fears how the war is changing the Jedi— particularly Padawans sent into war without enough training.

PLO KOON

A tough Kel Dor Jedi, Plo Koon is a skilled duelist and pilot. He is devoted to his clone squad, the Wolfpack. Plo has known Ahsoka all her life, and keeps an eye on the Padawan he calls "Little 'Soka".

SEPARATIST MASTERMIND

THE CONFEDERACY OF Independent Systems, or CIS, says that its goal is to free corporations, trade groups, and plane from the grip of the corrupt Galactic Senate. Many planetar leaders believe in that cause wholeheartedly. But the Separatist leadership has a secret agenda. The public lead of the movement, Count Dooku, is the apprentice of a mysterious Sith Lord who seeks to use the dark side of the Force to take over the Senate, destroy the Jedi Order, and rule the galaxy.

PUBLIC LEADER

The charismatic Count Dooku was once a Jedi Master, but left the Order to return to his wealthy homeworld of Serenno. Dooku has studied the dark arts of the Sith and now holds the secret title Darth Tyranus.

SEPARATIST PAWNS

The Sith pursue their plot to defeat the Republic and take over the galaxy on many worlds, seeking allies among rebels, banned groups, and defeated movements. One of their many pawns is Pre Vizsla, leader of the Mandalorian Death Watch.

CYBORG GENERAL

The Separatists' military commander is General Grievous, a Kaleesh warlord who has replaced most of his living flesh with mechanical parts. Grievous has destroyed many Republic worlds. His name causes fear across the galaxy.

SECRET MASTER

The Republic has heard the name Darth Sidious—Count Dooku himself told Obi-Wan Kenobi about the Sith Lord who had taken over the Senate. Obi-Wan didn't believe him, and neither do the intelligence officials who serve Chancellor Palpatine. But Dooku wasn't lying. Sidious exists and is the secret mastermind behind the Separatist war effort and the Sith plot.

AN OLD FLAME

Clovis is still in love with Padmé and jumps at the chance to rekindle their romance, inviting her on a trip to Cato Neimoidia with him.

TATTOOS ARE
A MARK OF
STATUS

RUSH CLOVIS

RUSH CLOVIS REPRESENTS Scipio in the Senate and is a high-ranking member of the Banking Clan. The Jedi suspect him of being a Separatist sympathizer and send Padmé Amidala—with whom Clovis had a long-ago romance—to determine where the charismatic, wealthy young baron's loyalties truly lie.

TUNIC
DECORATED TO
LOOK LIKE
ARMOR

CATO NEIMOIDIA

Cato Neimoidia is a purse-world of the greedy Neimoidians who dominate the Trade Federation. The lush planet is reserved for their wealthiest nobles. Sitting in their luxurious palaces, they plot to destroy the Republic. While the Republic has been battered by the war, Neimoidians have suffered too. They have signed over much of their wealth to Banking Clan nobles such as Clovis, who use it as collateral for loans to build new armies and warships that Count Dooku requires for the war.

THE SENATOR'S SCHEME

When Clovis impulsively brings Padmé to Cato Neimoidia, Lott Dod slips her poison. His plan is to trade Clovis the antidote in exchange for better terms on the Banking Clan's loan. It's a perfect scheme: If Clovis accepts, Dod saves credits. If he declines, an old enemy of the Trade Federation dies.

LOTT DOD

Lott Dod is the Trade Federation's Senator who continues to serve on Coruscant despite the fact that everyone knows he is a high-ranking Separatist. Dod does his part to keep up this fiction, retreating to Cato Neimoidia to do business with his fellow Separatists away from the eyes of Republic Intelligence and other spies.

CREDIT CRISIS

★ Many in the Banking Clan and other megacorporations support the Separatists. But although they take orders from Dooku, the corporations are vital to the galactic economy, and so the Senate reluctantly looks the other way and ignores their treasonous acts.

FORBIDDEN LOVE

THE JEDI AREN'T ALLOWED to romantically connect with others, as attachments can lead to jealousy, anger, and the pull of the dark side of the Force. But human nature is hard to fight. Anakin Skywalker has ignored the code with his secret marriage to Padmé Amidala, and Obi-Wan Kenobi has never forgotten his affection for Duchess Satine.

STOLEN MOMENTS

Between war in countless star systems and the business of the Senate, Anakin and Padmé have few opportunities to enjoy a quiet evening alone in each other's company.

"I BROUGHT DINNER"

Anakin has to hitch a ride to Coruscant on a freighter, but the captain offers him a gift: khasva rolls from Mon Calamari. Pair them with five-blossom bread from Naboo and you have a romantic dinner.

JEDI CHOICES

Anakin has never told Obi-Wan of his marriage to Padmé, and is surprised to learn his former Master has struggled with attachments of his own. He asks Obi-Wan how he was able to ignore his feelings for Duchess Satine. Obi-Wan replies that he lives by the Jedi Code. Despite this, Anakin can see that Obi-Wan still has deep regrets.

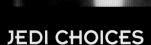

STRONG FEELINGS

Obi-Wan Kenobi and Satine Kryze are an odd pair: a Jedi skilled in combat arts and a pacifist born to Kalevalan royalty. But opposites attract and beneath their quarrels lies a lifelong affection.

DANGER!

As a Padawan, Obi-Wan risked his life to save Satine from foes on Mandalore. Now he must do the same on Coruscant.

C-3PO

RECHARGE SOCKET

☒ As a boy on Tatooine, Anakin Skywalker built C-3PO using parts from junked droids. It was a lowly beginning for C-3PO, who now serves Padmé Amidala on Senate business. He has acquired shiny gold plating more suitable for diplomatic affairs.

R2-D2

LOGIC DISPLAY

SYSTEM VENT

☆ A spirited, stubborn astromech, R2-D2 was once the property of the Royal House of Naboo, but now serves Anakin Skywalker on dangerous missions. The young Jedi thinks of R2 as a friend, and refuses to wipe the little droid's electronic memory.

BETTY DROIDS

☆ BD-3000 droids are graceful, gleaming robots that come in a variety of bright hues. They are common on Coruscant, where they serve the wealthy as secretaries and butlers.

COMPUTER BRAIN

BALANCE SENSORS

INJECTION SYRINGE

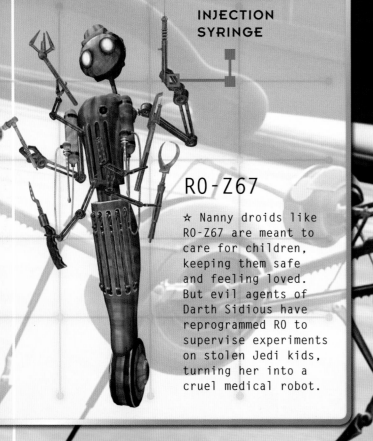

RO-Z67

☆ Nanny droids like RO-Z67 are meant to care for children, keeping them safe and feeling loved. But evil agents of Darth Sidious have reprogrammed RO to supervise experiments on stolen Jedi kids, turning her into a cruel medical robot.

ANTENNAE

STORAGE IN BODY

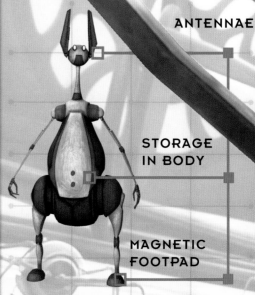

MAGNETIC FOOTPAD

LEP DROIDS

☆ Originally designed for childcare, these small droids have proven useful as valets and assistants, waddling behind their owners, waiting for an errand or small task.

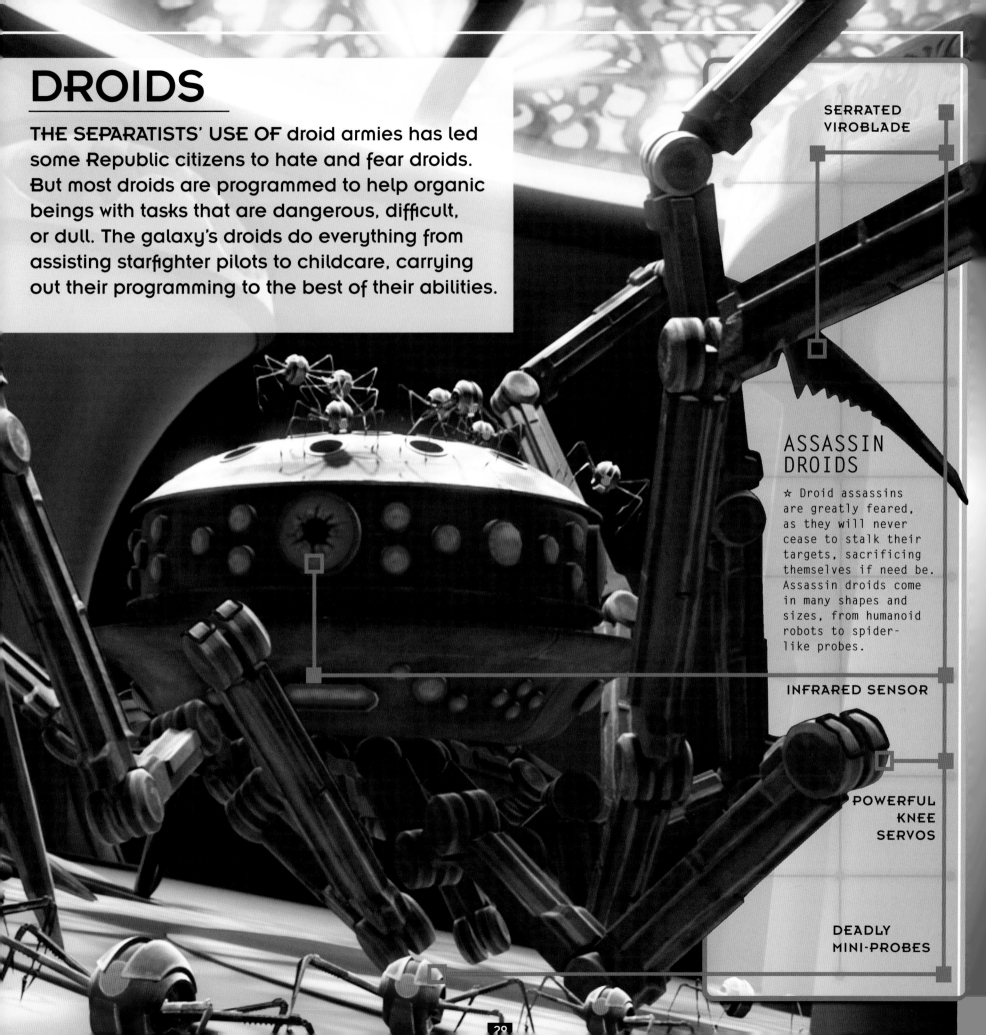

DROIDS

THE SEPARATISTS' USE OF droid armies has led some Republic citizens to hate and fear droids. But most droids are programmed to help organic beings with tasks that are dangerous, difficult, or dull. The galaxy's droids do everything from assisting starfighter pilots to childcare, carrying out their programming to the best of their abilities.

SERRATED VIROBLADE

ASSASSIN DROIDS

☆ Droid assassins are greatly feared, as they will never cease to stalk their targets, sacrificing themselves if need be. Assassin droids come in many shapes and sizes, from humanoid robots to spider-like probes.

INFRARED SENSOR

POWERFUL KNEE SERVOS

DEADLY MINI-PROBES

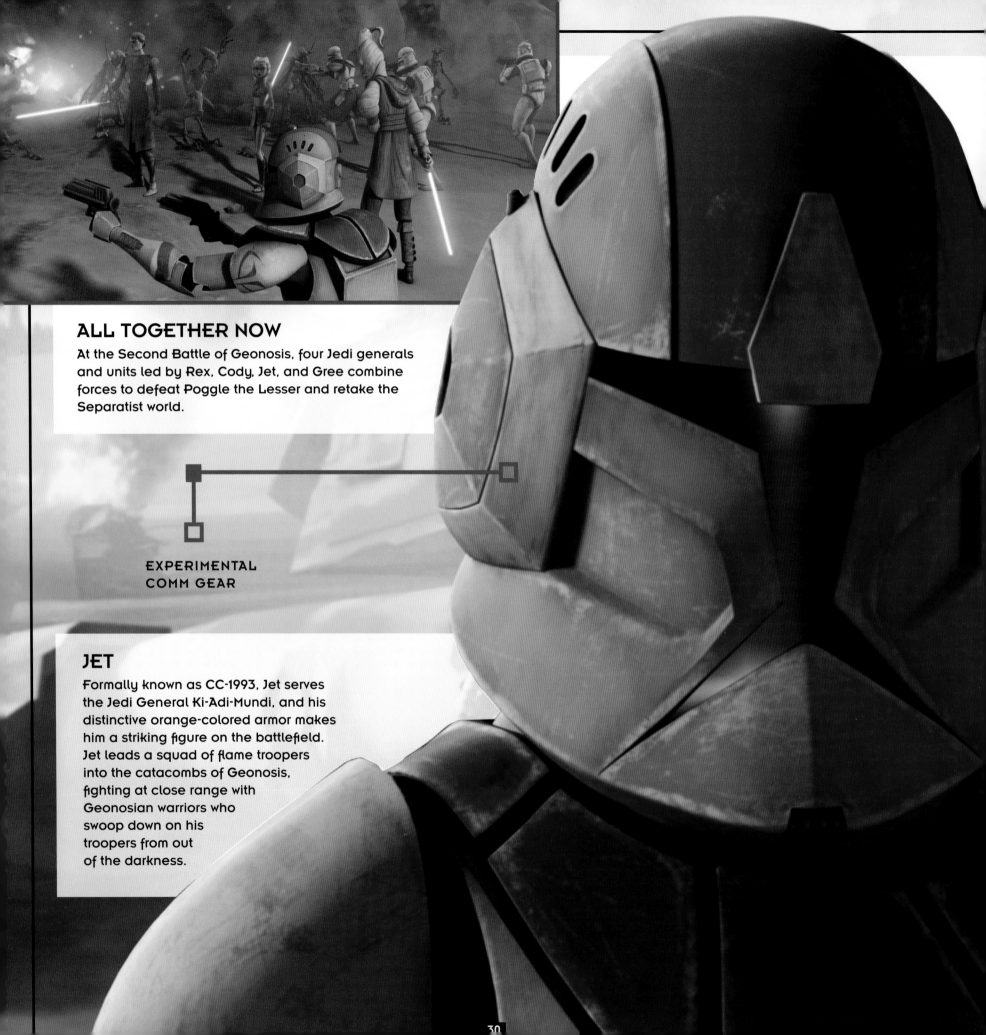

ALL TOGETHER NOW

At the Second Battle of Geonosis, four Jedi generals and units led by Rex, Cody, Jet, and Gree combine forces to defeat Poggle the Lesser and retake the Separatist world.

EXPERIMENTAL COMM GEAR

JET

Formally known as CC-1993, Jet serves the Jedi General Ki-Adi-Mundi, and his distinctive orange-colored armor makes him a striking figure on the battlefield. Jet leads a squad of flame troopers into the catacombs of Geonosis, fighting at close range with Geonosian warriors who swoop down on his troopers from out of the darkness.

CLONE COMMANDERS

THE JEDI COMMAND the Republic's clone armies, but the Order has too few generals to direct all the troops. Filling the gaps are non-Jedi officers and clones, who are identified early in the growth process on Kamino as promising officer candidates. These clones receive specialized training in leadership and tactics and are programmed to use their initiative. The best officers serve alongside Jedi generals.

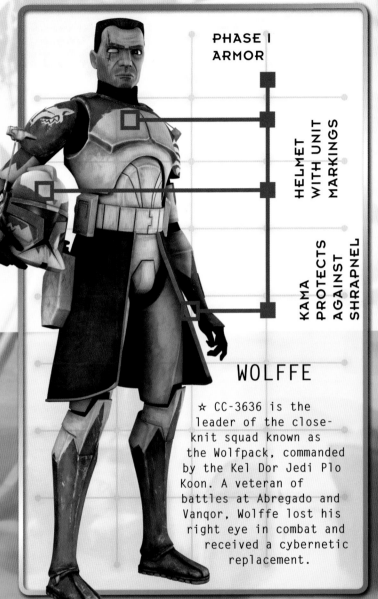

PHASE I
ARMOR

HELMET WITH UNIT MARKINGS

KAMA PROTECTS AGAINST SHRAPNEL

LOCK

A captain in Horn Company, CC-4142 fights alongside Eeth Koth. When Grievous attacks the *Steadfast* near Arda, Lock leads the Jedi Cruiser's defense before obeying Koth's order to evacuate in an escape pod.

DISTINCTIVE ORANGE ARMOR

WOLFFE

✩ CC-3636 is the leader of the close-knit squad known as the Wolfpack, commanded by the Kel Dor Jedi Plo Koon. A veteran of battles at Abregado and Vanqor, Wolffe lost his right eye in combat and received a cybernetic replacement.

CODY

Second-in-command to Obi-Wan Kenobi, CC-2224, or "Cody" is a cautious but extremely effective soldier. Cody and Rex have grown close over several dangerous campaigns, and Cody worries that Rex's willingness to rush into battle will one day prove fatal.

REX

A gruff, no-nonsense soldier, CC-7567 serves Anakin Skywalker and shares his Jedi general's bravery and occasional recklessness in battle. His helmet is adorned with Jaig Eyes—a battle honor assigned by the Mandalorian veterans who train clone officers on Kamino.

REPUBLIC FORCES

TO COUNTER THE Separatist onslaught, factory worlds across the Republic are busy turning out warships, starfighters, and ground vehicles for deployment on many worlds. This military buildup is new: For centuries, the Republic had no centralized military, preferring to use warriors and warships drawn from individual star systems. Now, Jedi generals lead a Grand Army and Navy against Count Dooku's forces.

HEAVY CANNON

AT-TEs

☆ AT-TEs pack a punch, blasting targets with six laser cannons and a missile launcher. They carry clone troopers to the front lines, using foot grips and magnetic toes to climb slopes or cliffs. Specialized gunships fly AT-TEs to the battlefield.

LAAT/i GUNSHIPS

MISSILE LAUNCHER

☆ LAAT/i gunships can carry an entire platoon of clone troopers in their bellies at speeds topping 600 kilometers an hour. They protect their cargo with blast cannons, laser guns, and twin missile launchers. Troopers like to name and decorate their gunships.

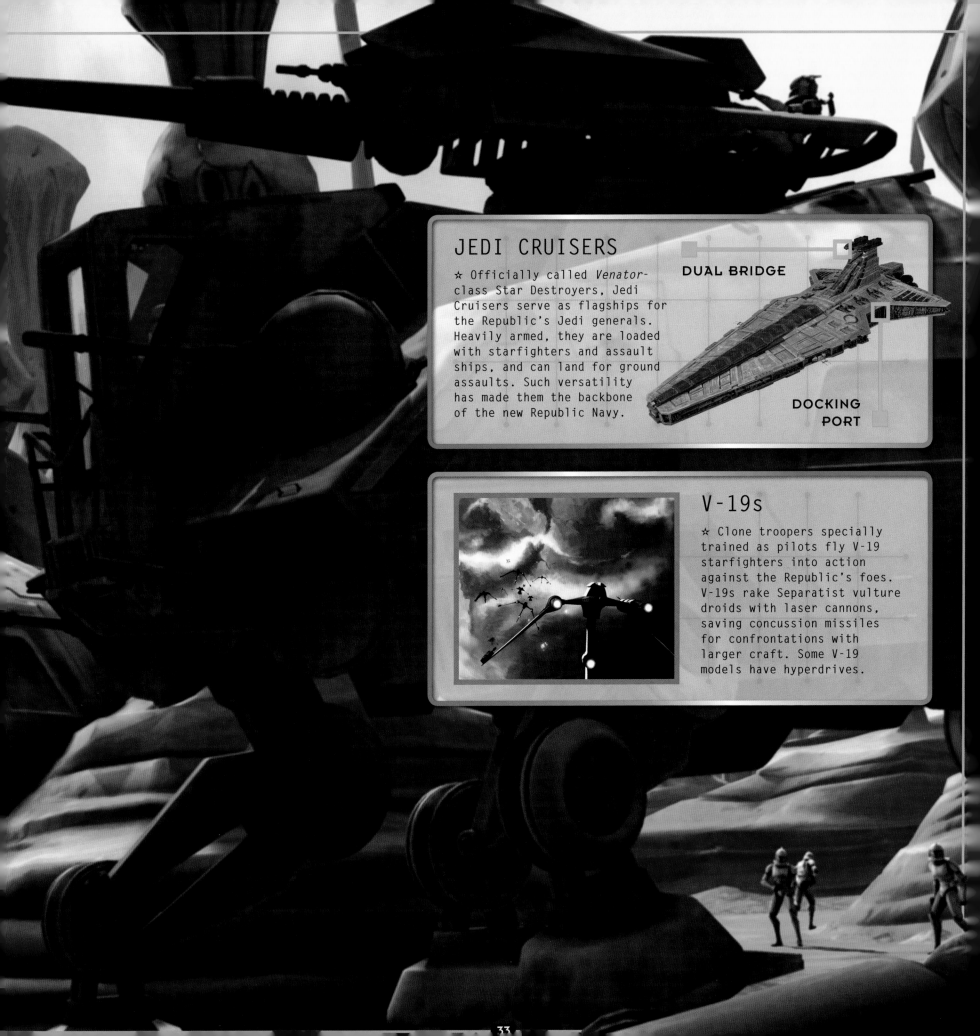

JEDI CRUISERS

☆ Officially called *Venator*-
class Star Destroyers, Jedi
Cruisers serve as flagships for
the Republic's Jedi generals.
Heavily armed, they are loaded
with starfighters and assault
ships, and can land for ground
assaults. Such versatility
has made them the backbone
of the new Republic Navy.

DUAL BRIDGE

DOCKING
PORT

V-19s

☆ Clone troopers specially
trained as pilots fly V-19
starfighters into action
against the Republic's foes.
V-19s rake Separatist vulture
droids with laser cannons,
saving concussion missiles
for confrontations with
larger craft. Some V-19
models have hyperdrives.

SEPARATIST ARMIES

THE METAL LEGIONS of the Separatists don't need food or water—just power and programming. In their billions, they have conquered thousands of worlds and threaten many more. Their forces include smart leaders such as tactical droids, dumb but tough Super Battle Droids, wily commandos, and ruthless droidekas. Clone troopers are smarter and better trained, but are fewer than their enemies.

SUPER BATTLE DROIDS

Super Battle Droids aren't smart, but they're so tough that they don't need big brains. The Separatists' heavy hitters, they rely on their thick armor and powerful laser cannons to bash through any resistance. Some models have built-in jetpacks that allow them to launch aerial assaults.

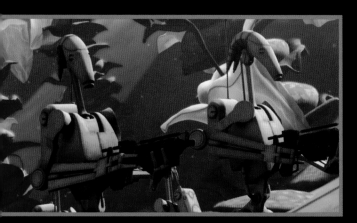

BATTLE DROIDS

These simple, sturdy machines overwhelm enemies through sheer numbers. By some Republic estimates quintillions have already been destroyed, but Separatist factories turn out more every day. Some battle droids have been reprogrammed to pilot ships, fight fires, and perform more complex functions. But they aren't very good at such tasks, to their commanders' annoyance.

BATTLE DROID COMMANDERS

Distinguished by yellow markings, battle droid commanders download extensive orders for use in battles. They take pride in their status and like to boss around regular battle droids, though they're actually no smarter.

TACTICAL DROIDS

These droid leaders boast state-of-the-art computer brains and use them to study their enemies to improve their chances of victory. They look down on living beings for their illogical emotions.

ENERGY SHIELD

PRIMARY SENSOR

TWIN BLASTERS

FLEXIBLE MIDSECTION

DROIDEKAS

☆ Also known as destroyer droids, these deadly mechanicals roll into battle with their heads and legs curled into a wheel. They then unfurl, activate their energy shields and begin blasting away with their powerful laser cannons.

COMMANDO DRIODS

☆ Tough, smart, and fast, commando droids are a match for even veteran clone troopers. They carry several weapons, move quietly, and can mimic voices. Fortunately for the Republic, commando droids are expensive and remain rare sights on the battlefield.

FAST-SWITCH SERVOMOTORS

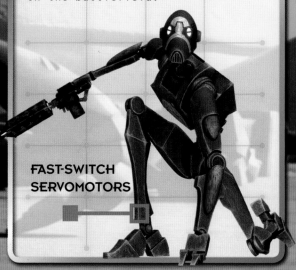

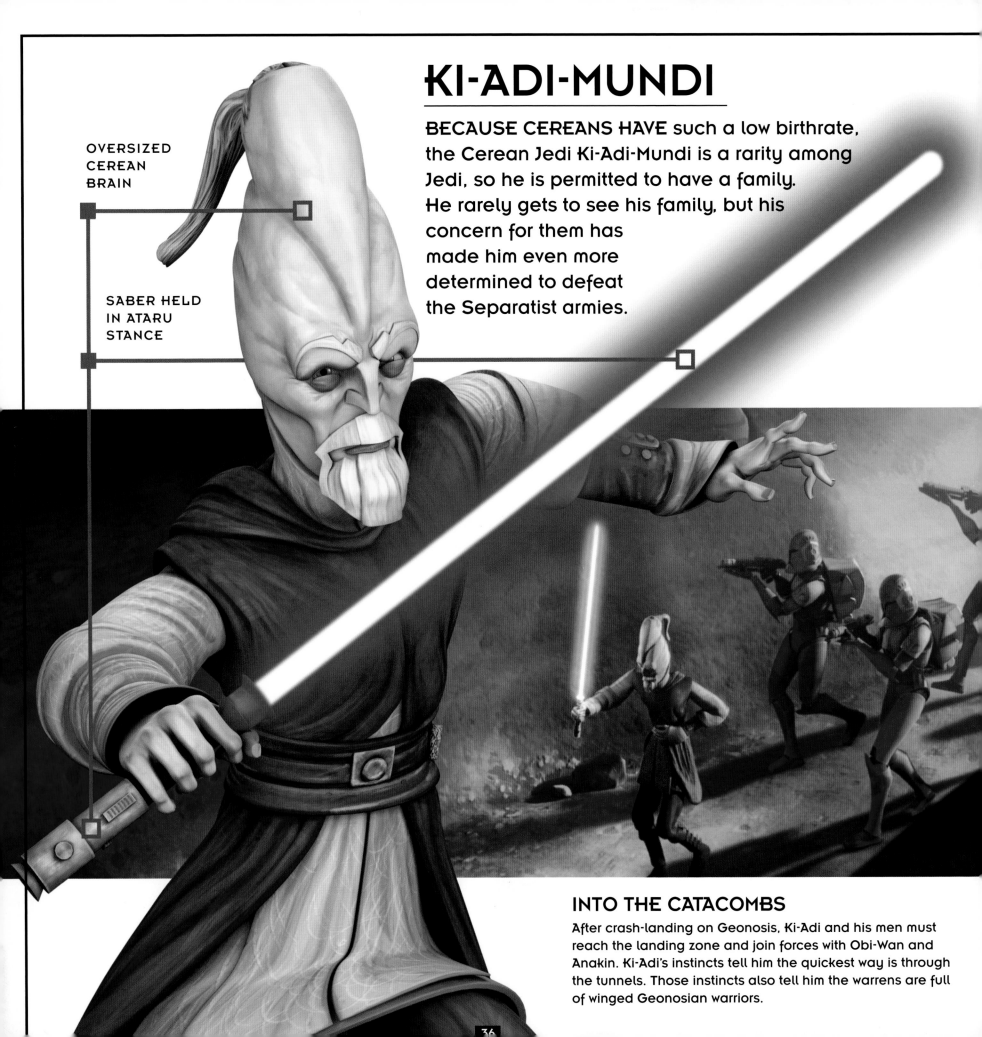

KI-ADI-MUNDI

BECAUSE CEREANS HAVE such a low birthrate, the Cerean Jedi Ki-Adi-Mundi is a rarity among Jedi, so he is permitted to have a family. He rarely gets to see his family, but his concern for them has made him even more determined to defeat the Separatist armies.

OVERSIZED
CEREAN
BRAIN

SABER HELD
IN ATARU
STANCE

INTO THE CATACOMBS

After crash-landing on Geonosis, Ki-Adi and his men must reach the landing zone and join forces with Obi-Wan and Anakin. Ki-Adi's instincts tell him the quickest way is through the tunnels. Those instincts also tell him the warrens are full of winged Geonosian warriors.

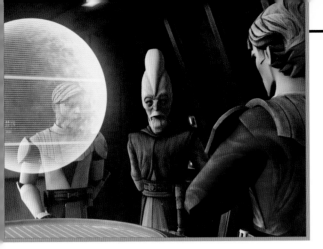

RETURN TO GEONOSIS

After the First Battle of Geonosis, the Republic underestimated both the Geonosians' resistance and their loyalty to the Separatists. Now, Poggle the Lesser has rebuilt his droid foundries and is again aiding Count Dooku. Retaking the planet is essential to the Republic war effort.

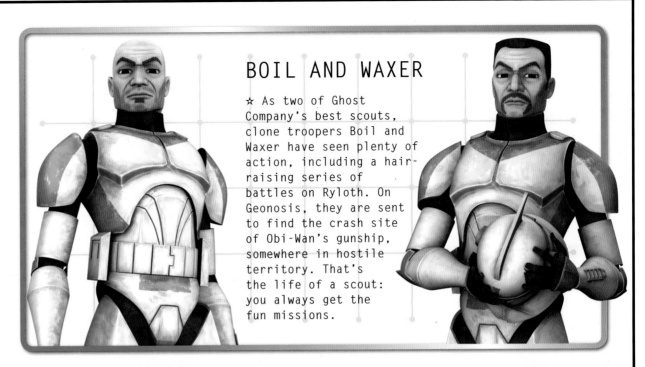

BOIL AND WAXER

☆ As two of Ghost Company's best scouts, clone troopers Boil and Waxer have seen plenty of action, including a hair-raising series of battles on Ryloth. On Geonosis, they are sent to find the crash site of Obi-Wan's gunship, somewhere in hostile territory. That's the life of a scout: you always get the fun missions.

MAKING HIS OWN LUCK

Ki-Adi was captured during the First Battle of Geonosis and is determined not to fail again. He and Commander Jet have spent hours studying intelligence reports about the planet's defenses and are ready for anything. When Admiral Yularen wishes him good luck, Ki-Adi says that there's no such thing.

WAR'S REWARD

With the Geonosians finally in retreat, the Republic's troops can target the shield generators protecting Poggle's droid foundry. As the tired Jedi regroup, Ki-Adi knows the battle for Geonosis has just begun.

CLONE TROOPERS

THE DEFENDERS OF the Republic are millions of clones genetically engineered for loyalty and bravery. Grown in vats on Kamino, the clones age much faster than humans, with young trainees selected for instruction as pilots, scouts, officers, and commandos. While often thought of as flesh-and-blood droids, clone troopers have the same hopes, dreams, and fears as non-cloned humans.

UNDER THE ARMOR

All clones train in standard body armor that is made up of 20 plastoid-alloy plates over a pressurized black body glove. However, troopers don specialized armor for different missions: Scouts' helmets are packed with sensors and pilots' body gloves are made for the high G-forces of spaceflight.

TAKING CHARGE

Kamino's cloners screen young clones for signs of leadership skills and the best candidates begin a rigorous training regime designed to turn them into leaders of their fellow troops. Clone officers show more initiative on the battlefield, and the Republic's Jedi generals have come to rely on men like Captain Rex during battles.

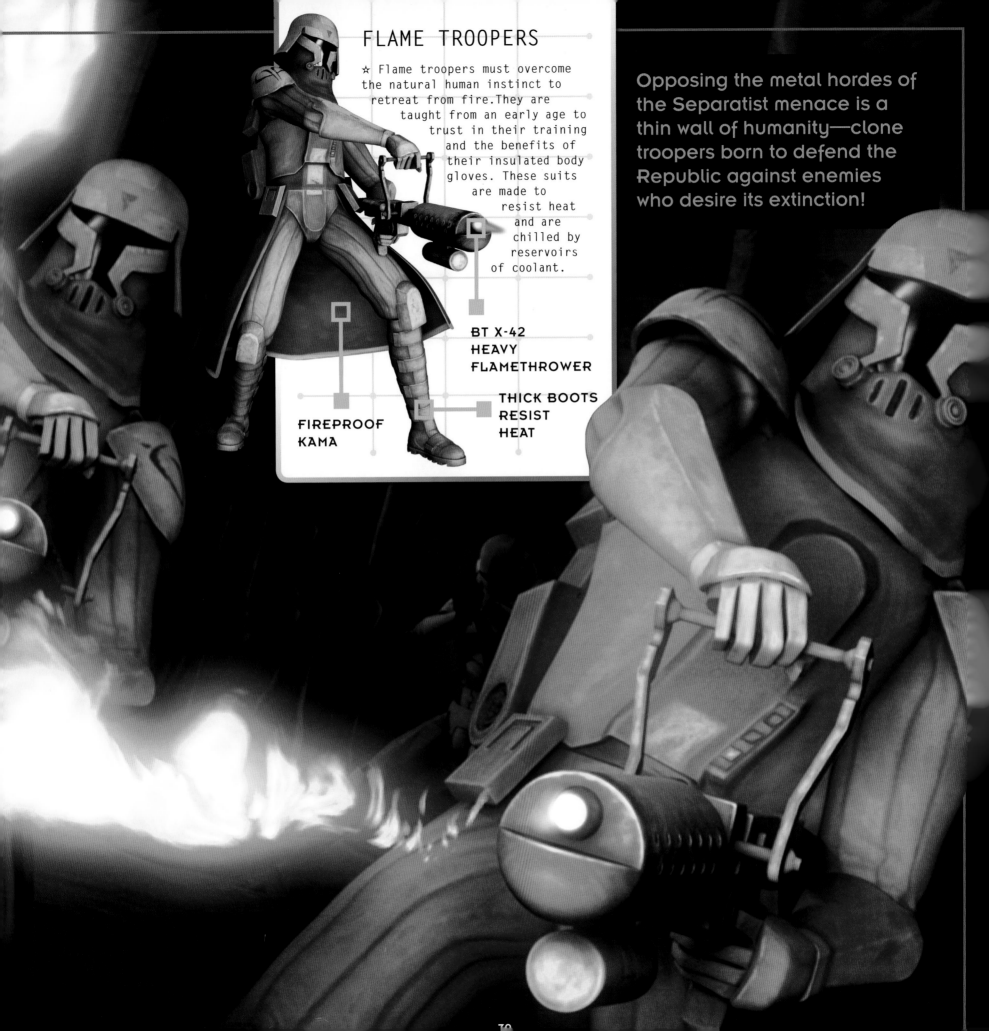

FLAME TROOPERS

★ Flame troopers must overcome the natural human instinct to retreat from fire. They are taught from an early age to trust in their training and the benefits of their insulated body gloves. These suits are made to resist heat and are chilled by reservoirs of coolant.

BT X-42 HEAVY FLAMETHROWER

FIREPROOF KAMA

THICK BOOTS RESIST HEAT

Opposing the metal hordes of the Separatist menace is a thin wall of humanity—clone troopers born to defend the Republic against enemies who desire its extinction!

"DON'T STOP! WE MUST PUSH ON!"

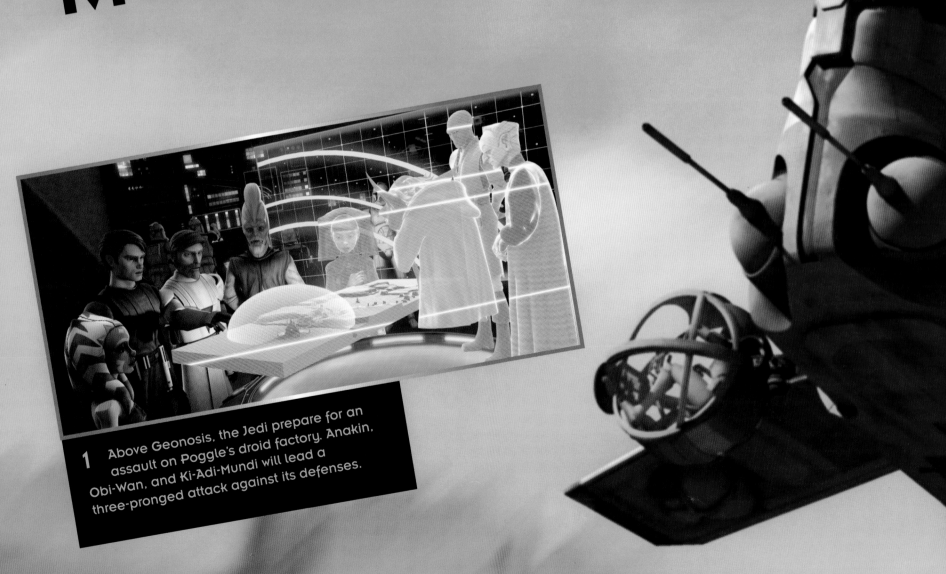

1 Above Geonosis, the Jedi prepare for an assault on Poggle's droid factory. Anakin, Obi-Wan, and Ki-Adi-Mundi will lead a three-pronged attack against its defenses.

2 Geonosians shoot down the three Jedi gunships, forcing Jedi and clones to fight their way across the desert. Atop a fortress wall, Anakin and Ahsoka battle droidekas!

3 When the three Jedi finally rendezvous, Anakin must help an injured Obi-Wan walk to the strategy meeting. The battle to land on Geonosis is only beginning!

POGGLE THE LESSER

POGGLE THE LESSER is the Archduke of Geonosis and one of the most committed supporters of the Separatist cause. He is also a high-ranking member of the Techno Union, and believes that aiding Count Dooku will give Geonosis and its hives of clever engineers the wealth and power they deserve. He also hopes to have his revenge against the Republic for occupying his planet and destroying many of its factories.

TRUE BELIEVER

To Poggle, not all Separatists are equal. For instance, he hates the InterGalactic Banking Clan's Rush Clovis, who seems more interested in his own profits than in the Republic's defeat.

HIVE MIND

Geonosian society relies upon the work of wingless drones who support winged warriors and the royal castes. At the pinnacle of this insect hierarchy sits the mysterious, hidden Geonosian queen.

Geonosians

☆ The winged caste of Geonosian warriors live to serve their hives, sacrificing themselves without a moment's thought if ordered to do so. While they have little sense of themselves as individuals, they are smart fighters, and clone troopers fear their deadly sonic blasters.

LAST DEFENSE

Poggle's new factories are ringed with shield generators and defended by Geonosians and droids. But a wise Geonosian always has a backup plan—Poggle is to flee to the secret lair of his true ruler.

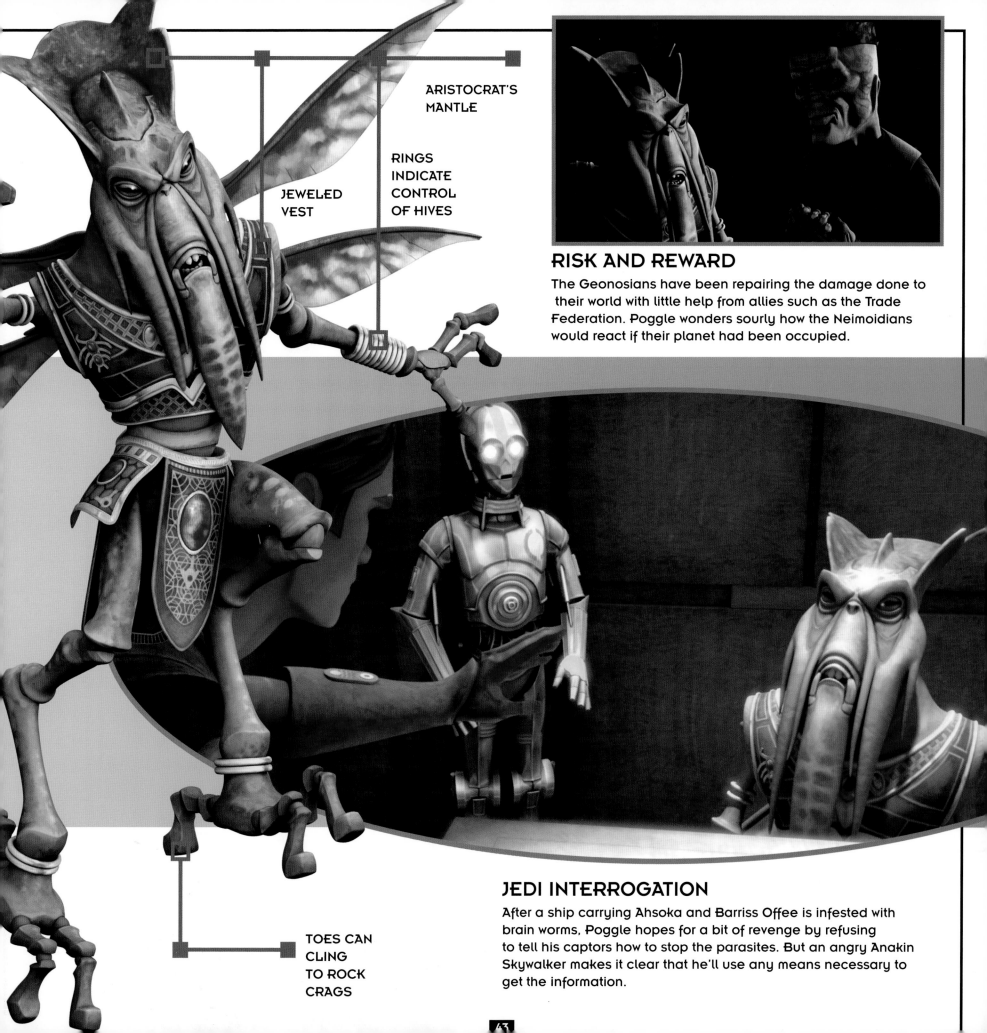

ARISTOCRAT'S MANTLE

JEWELED VEST

RINGS INDICATE CONTROL OF HIVES

RISK AND REWARD

The Geonosians have been repairing the damage done to their world with little help from allies such as the Trade Federation. Poggle wonders sourly how the Neimoidians would react if their planet had been occupied.

TOES CAN CLING TO ROCK CRAGS

JEDI INTERROGATION

After a ship carrying Ahsoka and Barriss Offee is infested with brain worms, Poggle hopes for a bit of revenge by refusing to tell his captors how to stop the parasites. But an angry Anakin Skywalker makes it clear that he'll use any means necessary to get the information.

BARRISS OFFEE

BARRISS OFFEE SERVES Luminara Unduli as an apprentice and is a model Padawan: loyal, obedient, and responsible. So it's a bit of a surprise when Barriss becomes friends with Ahsoka Tano, the rebellious, wisecracking apprentice of Anakin Skywalker. While the two Padawans seem very different, both are committed to the Jedi Order and are determined to learn how to use the Force for the good of the Republic and its people.

MIRIALAN TATTOOS

SABER LOOKS LIKE LUMINARA'S

BELT MADE OF NERF HIDE

NOT HERSELF

Barriss and Ahsoka join Tango Company for a trip to Ord Cestus aboard medical frigate TB-73. But brain worms infect the clone troopers and eventually Barriss. Possessed by the worms, Barriss hunts Ahsoka with her lightsaber.

SLOW AND STEADY

On Geonosis, Barriss and Ahsoka cut their way into the catacombs beneath Poggle the Lesser's droid foundry. Their mission is to find a way through the labyrinth of passageways to set explosives and blow the foundry to bits. Barriss says she has memorized each twist and turn of the maze. But practice doesn't always make perfect.

BAD EXAMPLE

Luminara Unduli doesn't approve of Ahsoka's disobedience or the way Anakin argues publicly with his apprentice. As Luminara sees it, a Padawan's job is to follow orders—and arguing in public can hurt morale. Barriss agrees with her Master—but she can't help wondering what it would be like to disagree so openly with her own teacher.

SHOCKING DEVELOPMENT

After brain worms infect the medical frigate, it's impossible for Barriss and Ahsoka to tell friend from foe. The clone troopers of Tango Company know the Jedi and their weaknesses, and stun Barriss with an electrical trap.

THE TOOLS OF SUCCESS

Luminara has no doubt that Barriss will do her part to ensure a Republic victory on Geonosis. She has taught Barriss that to succeed, you must prepare well—particularly when people are depending on you.

SUPER TANKS

☆ A prototype vehicle built by the Baktoid Armor Workshop, the Super Tank is seen as an improvement on the MTT troop transport, adding an armor shell that can withstand most things Republic forces throw at it. The shell retracts to reveal two powerful missile launchers.

SEPARATIST FORCES

THE SEPARATISTS DRAW their military might from planets and large companies that tried to leave the Republic and have now joined forces to defeat its armies and navies. The members of the Confederacy of Independent Systems are expected to contribute droid armies, vehicles, and warships as needed. Gigantic factories have sprung up on Separatist worlds as well as on planets seized from the Republic.

TRADE FEDERATION BATTLESHIPS

☆ *Lucrehulk*-class battleships were freighters for the Trade Federation used for hauling goods along the galaxy's trade routes. The Neimoidians refitted them as warships to guard their cargos from pirates on the Outer Rim. They now carry both droid armies and fighter squadrons.

BANKING CLAN FRIGATES

COMMAND BRIDGE

☆ Originally used by the Banking Clan to guard its vaults and threaten worlds that wouldn't pay their debts, these spear-shaped warships now make up the bulk of the Separatist navy. They can carry 150,000 battle droids in their vast holds, defending them with laser cannons.

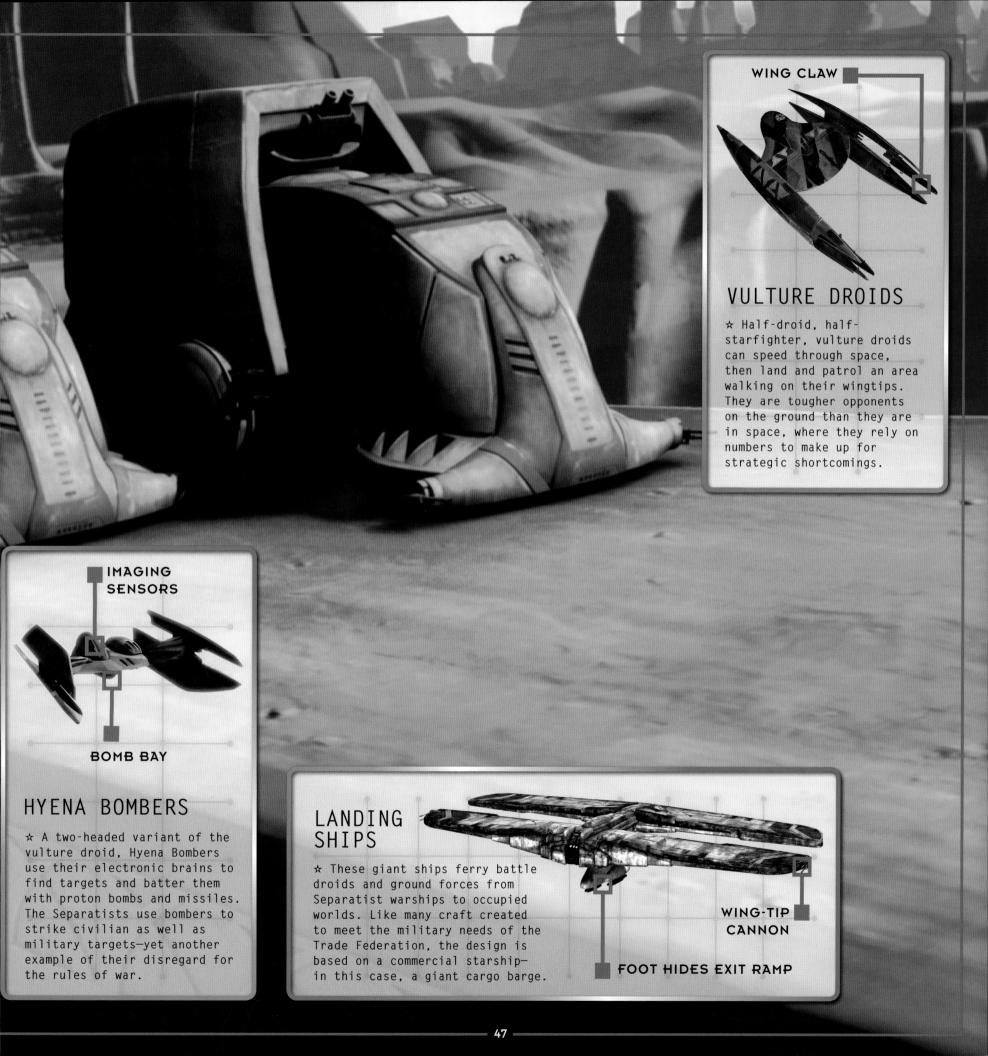

WING CLAW

VULTURE DROIDS

☆ Half-droid, half-starfighter, vulture droids can speed through space, then land and patrol an area walking on their wingtips. They are tougher opponents on the ground than they are in space, where they rely on numbers to make up for strategic shortcomings.

IMAGING SENSORS

BOMB BAY

HYENA BOMBERS

☆ A two-headed variant of the vulture droid, Hyena Bombers use their electronic brains to find targets and batter them with proton bombs and missiles. The Separatists use bombers to strike civilian as well as military targets—yet another example of their disregard for the rules of war.

LANDING SHIPS

☆ These giant ships ferry battle droids and ground forces from Separatist warships to occupied worlds. Like many craft created to meet the military needs of the Trade Federation, the design is based on a commercial starship— in this case, a giant cargo barge.

WING-TIP CANNON

FOOT HIDES EXIT RAMP

BATTLE AT THE BRIDGE

In an effort to buy time for their Padawans to infiltrate Poggle's droid factory and destroy it, Anakin and Luminara lead a frontal attack that draws out Poggle's forces. Can they give Ahsoka and Barriss enough time to complete their mission?

"SORRY, MASTER! WE CAN'T MAKE IT OUT."

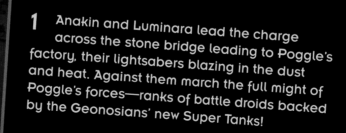

1 Anakin and Luminara lead the charge across the stone bridge leading to Poggle's factory, their lightsabers blazing in the dust and heat. Against them march the full might of Poggle's forces—ranks of battle droids backed by the Geonosians' new Super Tanks!

2 After luring the droids across the span, Anakin and Luminara use the Force to set explosive charges beneath it, hoping to send the deadly droids plummeting to their doom at the bottom of a chasm!

3 As the Jedi listen in horror, Ahsoka and Barriss say they're trapped in the factory and must sacrifice themselves to complete their task. A vast explosion destroys Poggle's factory—with the Padawans still inside!

4 Luminara accepts the grim news, but Anakin refuses to believe the Padawans are dead. He urges Luminara to help him use the Force to dig through the rubble!

SANDSTORM

Luminara Unduli and Buzz track a fleeing Poggle through a blinding sandstorm to the Progate Temple, unaware that they are about to stumble upon Karina's secret lair. Luminara is captured, and the Jedi must wait for the storm to pass before trying a rescue.

TRAPPINGS OF HIVE ROYALTY

KARINA THE GREAT

THE SECRET QUEEN of the Geonosian hives, Karina the Great dwells in the catacombs beneath the Progate Temple, from which she directs servants such as Poggle the Lesser. Karina uses parasites known as brain worms to control the minds of captured enemies, and gain access to their knowledge and memories. She hopes to regain the advantage in her planet's war with the Republic by infesting Jedi Knights with brain worms, giving her powerful new slaves who know the Republic's plans.

THE UNDEAD

☆ Brain worms are a powerful part of the Geonosian hive mind. They can animate the empty exoskeletons of dead Geonosians as a defense force against those who threaten the hive.

DUEL IN THE DARK

Obi-Wan, Anakin and their troopers descend into the catacombs in search of Luminara and find themselves battling hordes of undead Geonosians, who move silently in the pitch-black tunnels, strike without warning, and are barely slowed by laser blasts.

CROWN OF THE GEONOSIAN HIVES

QUEEN'S VESTIGIAL CLAWS ARE ALL BUT USELESS

EGG SAC HEAVY WITH NEW DRONES

THE QUEEN'S CHAMBER

At the heart of the catacombs lies Karina's royal chamber, where the giant queen lays her eggs and is tended by her retinue of Geonosian servants. As far as the Jedi know, no outsider has ever seen this place, or stood face-to-face with a Geonosian queen. Despite their perilous situation, Obi-Wan is fascinated by this latest mystery of the galaxy.

BENEATH THE TEMPLE

1 In the darkness beneath the Progate Temple, zombie Geonosian warriors attack the clone troopers. A blaster is no good when your enemy is already dead!

2 Luminara hopes her friends obeyed her warning to stay away. Karina the Great plans to use her brain worms to take over Anakin and Obi-Wan's minds!

On a mission to find Luminara Unduli, Anakin and Obi-Wan discover a terrible secret in the Geonosian catacombs.

3 Anakin and Obi-Wan rescue Luminara from the Geonosian queen. But now they must fight their way back to the planet's surface!

4 Leading Poggle as their prisoner, the Jedi flee the temple as the mighty structure begins to topple with a roar of tumbling stone!

STAND DOWN

After they're attacked in the mess hall, Ahsoka and Barriss don't trust anyone with a gun. But Trap and Havoc put down their weapons, so they must not be infected. Right?

TANGO COMPANY

AFTER A TOUGH FIGHT on Geonosis, Tango Company gets what sounds like an easy assignment: send a squad to protect a Republic frigate traveling to Ord Cestus to pick up medical supplies. But a dull mission turns deadly: One of Tango's troopers has been infected by a brain worm from Karina the Great's hive. He is carrying enough eggs to infect his comrades and the two Padawans on board. Karina may yet have revenge on her Republic conquerors.

PULSAR

CT-9521 lives for battle, and even awakens his squad by firing his blaster into the air. Pulsar isn't thrilled to hear that his squad's next assignment is to be a bunch of errand boys—there's a whole galaxy full of Separatists left to fight. But the clone Sergeant soon finds that his squad's mission is anything but routine.

SCYTHE

A brain worm infects CT-9544 while he's taking a nap in the ruins of the Progate Temple. Heeding his worm's orders, Scythe gathers a clutch of eggs and brings them aboard the medical frigate in his Republic backpack.

BRAIN INVADERS

Once they take possession of living hosts, Geonosian brain worms work together to eliminate any enemies and gain control of the environment. But the parasites can be cunning: Instead of attacking right away, they will often wait until the odds are in their favor or they can launch a surprise attack on an unwary foe.

EDGE

CT-9538 is one of the first clones infected by Scythe, and he joins Ox in trying to kill Ahsoka and Barriss. A stray mutation has given Edge pale blue eyes instead of the brown eyes of nearly all clone troopers.

HAVOC

CT-9529 has adorned his helmet with a yellow smiley face, but there's nothing friendly about Havoc when he's wielding his DC-15 rifle—as many Geonosian drones discovered during the fighting on their planet.

TRAP

A lieutenant in Tango Company, CL-9632 takes command of the squad sent to Ord Cestus, but quickly falls prey to brain worms and is killed by Barriss during a fierce struggle.

FRIEND AND FOE

1 Crossing lightsabers with her fellow Padawan, Ahsoka pleads with Barriss to resist the brain worm's influence. But Barriss is helpless—she must obey the worm!

2 Ahsoka realizes she can't win by fighting, and breaks off the attack. She will hide until she can figure out a way to disarm Barriss.

3 After Anakin tells Ahsoka that the worms can't handle the freezing temperatures, she uses her saber to rupture the ship's coolant system.

After their ship is invaded by brain worms, Ahsoka and Barriss Offee are hunted by clones whose minds have been taken over by the parasites. But things are about to get much worse: Barriss has been possessed too.

4 The worm possessing Barriss abandons its host, and Ahsoka cuts it in two. The padawans will recover—and Poggle's plan for revenge has been foiled!

EETH KOTH

JEDI MASTER Eeth Koth is a longtime member of the Jedi Council and a veteran of many battles against the enemies of the Republic. Koth was nearly killed at the first Battle of Geonosis, but escaped with his life was soon commanding a task force sent to hunt Separatists raiding the worlds of the Outer Rim.

LONG HAIR TIED BACK

SABRE HELD IN DEFENSIVE POSTURE

TENDER MERCIES

Koth's task force is patrolling near the Outer Rim world of Arda when General Grievous ambushes the vessels and storms Koth's Jedi Cruiser, the *Steadfast*. The Jedi and his troops try to repel Grievous's battle droids, but the cyborg warlord sends MagnaGuards and commando droids into the fight. Not even a Jedi of Koth's talents can beat those odds.

ZABRAKS

A humanoid species from Iridonia in the Mid Rim, Zabraks have horned heads and tattoos—common sights on many worlds. Other notable Zabraks include Darth Maul, the Jedi Agen Kolar, and the mercenary Sugi.

HORN COMPANY UNIT MARKINGS

ELECTRO-STAFF OF PHRIK ALLOY

SERVOS DRIVE TORSO & ARMS

LEGS ARMORED WITH DURANIUM

MAGNAGUARDS

☆ As a warlord on Kalee, General Grievous traveled with a band of elite bodyguards. When he joined the Separatists, Count Dooku had mechanical guards built for him. The MagnaGuards' tough armor and deadly electrostaffs make them scarily effective when fighting in a group.

DUEL WITH GRIEVOUS

Finding himself face to mask with Grievous, Koth calls the Separatist champion a murderer and a coward. If only he could face Grievous alone! But General Grievous isn't interested in giving his foes a chance for a fair fight.

BAITING THE TRAP

While Grievous broadcasts his capture of Koth to the Jedi Temple, Koth quietly indicates with his fingers that Grievous has taken him to the Saleucami system. Koth hopes that the Republic will send warships to destroy the general. Grievous also hopes the Jedi will come, and is using Koth as bait to attract the two Jedi he hates most of all: Obi-Wan Kenobi and Anakin Skywalker.

SHIEN STAR

Adi is a master of the Shien style of lightsaber combat, known for its distinctive reverse grip. Shien is effective against enemies wielding blasters, making it perfect for battling the Separatists' droid armies. But during the mission to rescue Eeth Koth, Adi chooses a traditional, defensive style.

ADI GALLIA

A THOLOTHIAN JEDI known for her diplomatic abilities as well as her skill with a lightsaber, Adi Gallia is a respected member of the Jedi Council. Her diplomatic contacts gave the Republic some of its first warnings that Nute Gunray's Trade Federation was stirring up trouble in the Outer Rim—a chain of events that led to the galaxy-wide war against the Separatists.

THOLOTH HEADDRESS

NERF-HIDE UTILITY BELT

SO CLOSE

Above Saleucami, Adi crosses sabers with Grievous and gains the upper hand in their duel. But a ruptured docking tube allows him to make yet another quick getaway.

JEDI TIES

Adi and Qui-Gon Jinn were good friends. The two Jedi went on several missions with their Padawans, Siri Tachi and Obi-Wan Kenobi. Now, Adi is proud to fight alongside Obi-Wan and the apprentice he trained, Anakin Skywalker. Through such connections, the Jedi Order maintains its traditions.

AGGRESSIVE NEGOTIATIONS

Adi knows that some of her fellow Jedi Council members have their doubts about Anakin Skywalker, considering the supposed Chosen One barely mature enough to be a Jedi Knight, let alone have a Padawan learner of his own. But Adi admires not only Anakin's abilities, but also the self-confidence with which he carries himself. Watching him in battle, she knows her old friend Qui-Gon Jinn would have been proud of him.

1 Adi Gallia is an expert test pilot, but she is happy to give Anakin the tough job of coming out of hyperspace in the middle of a battle and tucking a Jedi shuttle against Grievous's hull.

RESCUE MISSION

In a bid to rescue Eeth Koth and capture Grievous, the Jedi decide on a daring strike at Saleucami. While Obi-Wan engages Grievous's ships and lures the warlord into a saber duel, Anakin and Adi will slip aboard the Separatist destroyer and free Koth. It's a desperate gamble that will require some amazing flying even by Anakin's standards.

"ANY CLOSER AND WE'D BE FLYING DOWN HALLWAYS."

2 In Anakin's capable hands, the Jedi shuttle is soon docked with the Separatist destroyer—its crew upside-down but ready for their mission. Adi has to admit she's impressed. But for Anakin, it's all in a day's work.

1 Grievous corners Obi-Wan on the bridge with two MagnaGuards. Obi-Wan tricks one droid into zapping the other, then disables the remaining one with a well-aimed kick.

2 Preparing to cross sabers with Grievous, Obi-Wan has a question for his foe: Why is he happy as Dooku's errand boy? What does he have to gain from his service?

FATEFUL DUEL

The Jedi use Grievous's hatred of their Order to tempt him into a trap: While Anakin and Adi Gallia rescue Eeth Koth from Grievous's ship, Obi-Wan will lure the cyborg aboard his own cruiser and take him captive. But it is easier said than done.

3 Pressing his own attack, Grievous has a chillingly simple answer for Obi-Wan: He has the future to gain—a future where there are no Jedi.

"THE STORY OF OBI-WAN KENOBI ENDS HERE!"

CUT LAWQUANE

CUT LAWQUANE IS a deserter from the Republic's clone army, who has tried to make a new life for himself on the Outer Rim world of Saleucami. He has a family, a farm, and something to look forward to besides a lifetime of war. But Cut's life changes when the war he fled comes to his new homeworld and he must fight to defend the people he loves.

A NEW LIFE

It's been a long time since Cut fought the Separatists. But when commando droids attack his farm, he uses the training he received in the Republic Army.

FLEXIBLE LEKKU

SUU LAWQUANE

Life isn't easy when you're a Twi'lek woman raising two children alone. Suu did her best with Shaeeah and Jek, but she was grateful to meet Cut. She saw at once that he was a kind man who yearned for a family, and that he would do anything to keep his adopted children safe in a war-torn galaxy.

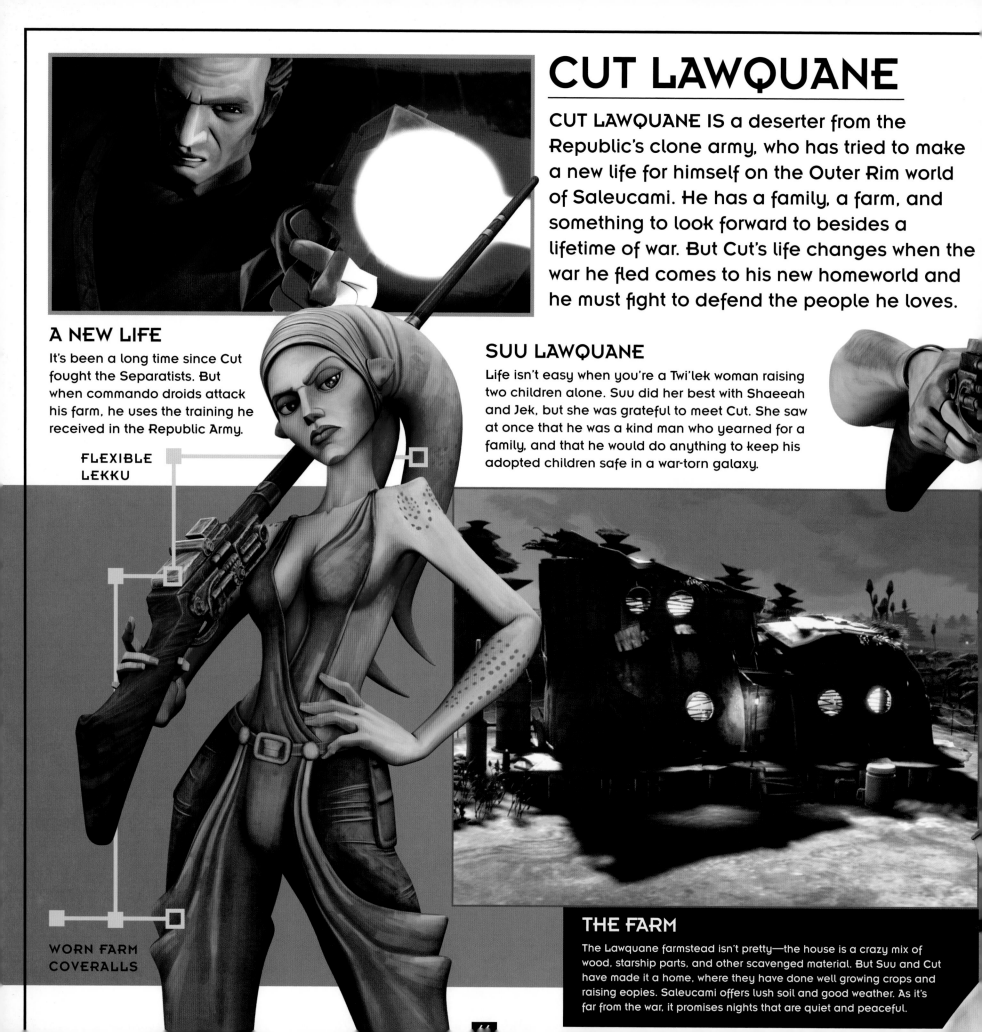

WORN FARM COVERALLS

THE FARM

The Lawquane farmstead isn't pretty—the house is a crazy mix of wood, starship parts, and other scavenged material. But Suu and Cut have made it a home, where they have done well growing crops and raising eopies. Saleucami offers lush soil and good weather. As it's far from the war, it promises nights that are quiet and peaceful.

SHAEEAH LAWQUANE

When Rex's troopers leave him in the barn, Suu tells her daughter to stay in the house. But the Twi'lek girl chases a toy into the barn and finds the wounded man. She is fascinated: Captain Rex looks just like her daddy.

ECOPIES

☆ Eopies are found on Tatooine and many other worlds. They are easy to domesticate, are adaptable to different climates and foods, and can pull heavy loads. The Lawquanes raise eopies for meat, milk, and hides, as well as beasts of burden on their farm.

ANTIQUE RIFLE

UTILITY POUCH

JEK LAWQUANE

Young Jek Lawquane notices the same thing his sister does: The man in their barn has the same face as their stepfather. But this doesn't trouble Jek: Surely it means their visitor is a friend, and friends always stay for dinner when they're visiting the farm. Captain Rex will eat dinner with them, right?

OUT OF ACTION

THE HUNT FOR General Grievous is interrupted when commando droids ambush Captain Rex's squad of troopers. A flash of light is the only warning before Rex tumbles from his speeder bike, felled by a laser blast to the chest. The hunt must continue, but Rex will have to sit out the mission while he heals.

CLOSE CALL

If the shot had come at closer range or been two inches to the left, the captain would not have survived. But it's bad enough: Kix, the unit's medic, needs to find a quiet place where he can tend to the injury without worrying about other droid snipers.

HELP, PLEASE!

Taking command, Jesse notices the squad is on farmland—and where there's a farm, there's a farmer. Following the fence, the clones find a homestead—and a wary Twi'lek woman with a big gun. Despite her worries, Suu Lawquane agrees to let Rex rest in the barn.

BARC SPEEDER USED BY CLONES

FAMILIAR FACE

Suu is kind to the injured Rex, but the clones sense something is bothering her. When her husband returns to the farm, Rex realizes what it is: Cut Lawquane is a fellow clone, a deserter from the clone army. Having escaped the war, Cut is not happy to see a familiar face.

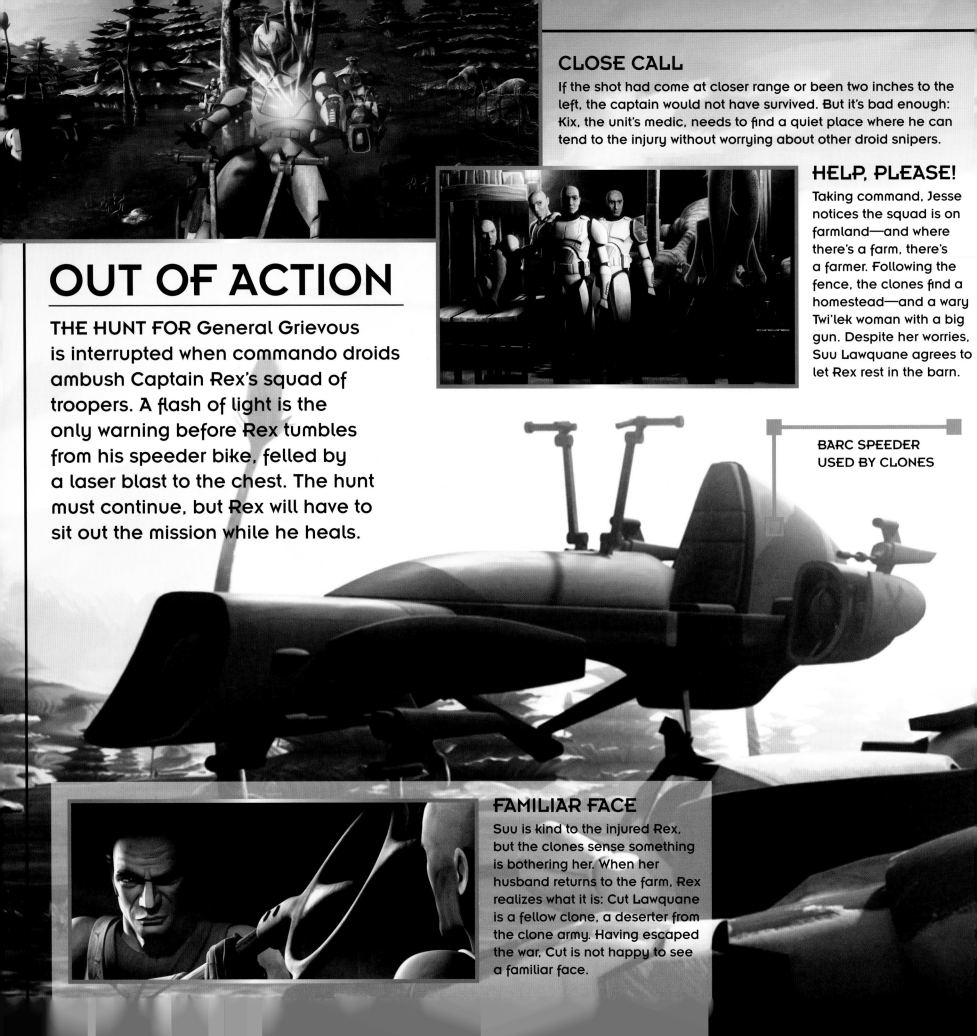

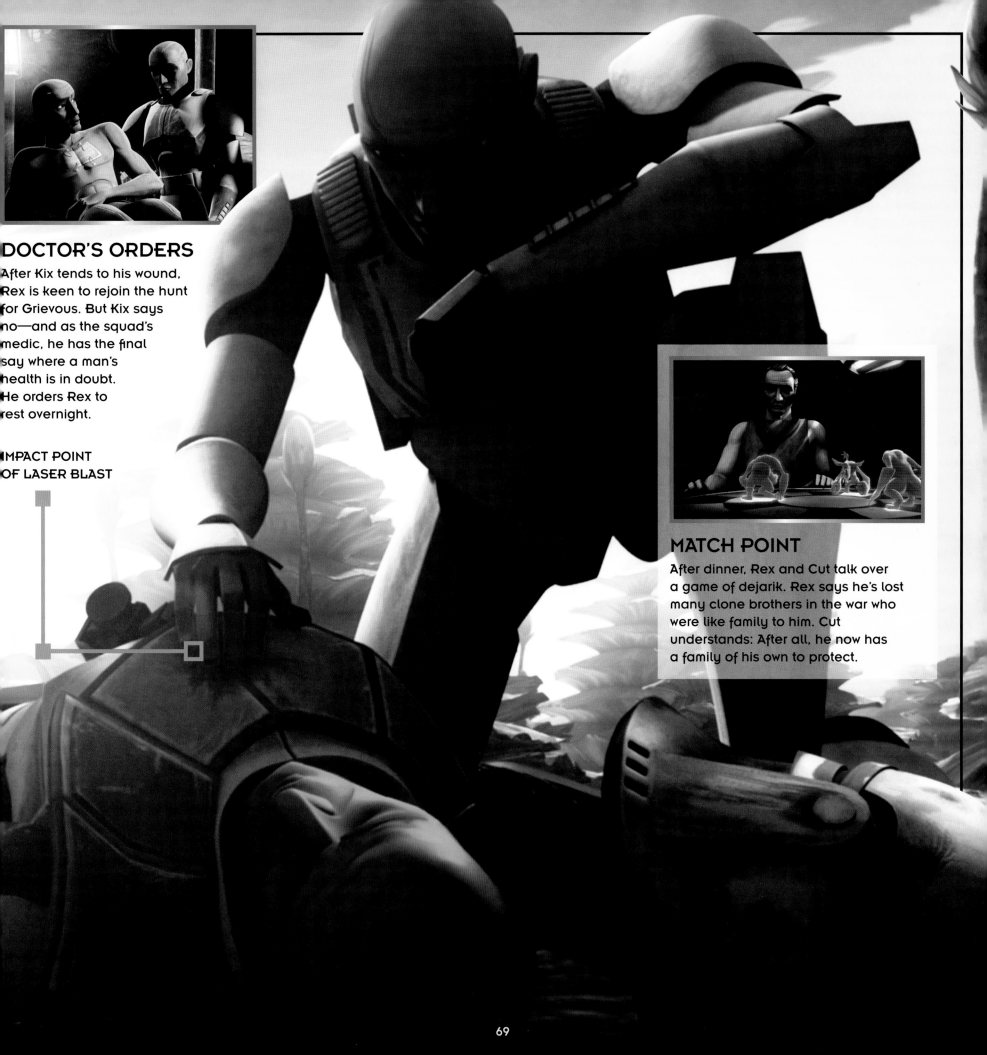

DOCTOR'S ORDERS

After Kix tends to his wound, Rex is keen to rejoin the hunt for Grievous. But Kix says no—and as the squad's medic, he has the final say where a man's health is in doubt. He orders Rex to rest overnight.

IMPACT POINT
OF LASER BLAST

MATCH POINT

After dinner, Rex and Cut talk over a game of dejarik. Rex says he's lost many clone brothers in the war who were like family to him. Cut understands: After all, he now has a family of his own to protect.

1 After finishing their evening chores, Jek and his sister Shaeeah stumble across an escape pod full of deadly commando droids.

HOMESTEAD INVASION

Cut Lawquane and his wife Suu offer Captain Rex a place to recover from his injuries. But other visitors to their farm are less friendly: Grievous's servants are prowling the night!

"MONSTERS! THEY'RE CHASING US!"

2 The children rush back to the house and hide upstairs with their mother. As the commando droids advance, Cut and Rex grab what weapons they have and prepare a desperate defense.

3 The commando droids are smart, fast, and sheathed in tough armor. But Rex is one of the best soldiers in the clone army. And Cut will stop at nothing to defend the people he loves.

TERA SINUBE

AN ELDERLY JEDI MASTER, Tera Sinube studies the Coruscant underworld and is familiar with many of the city-world's criminals. His skills as an investigator prove invaluable to Ahsoka Tano after a pickpocket steals her lightsaber. Sinube uses the Force, but like any good investigator, his most valuable skills are an ability to read people and anticipate their next move.

FIRST IMPRESSIONS

When Jedi librarian Jocasta Nu suggests that Ahsoka turn to Master Sinube for help recovering her lost lightsaber, Ahsoka isn't impressed: The Cosian Jedi is fast asleep. But Ahsoka soon finds that Sinube has much to teach her about wisdom and patience.

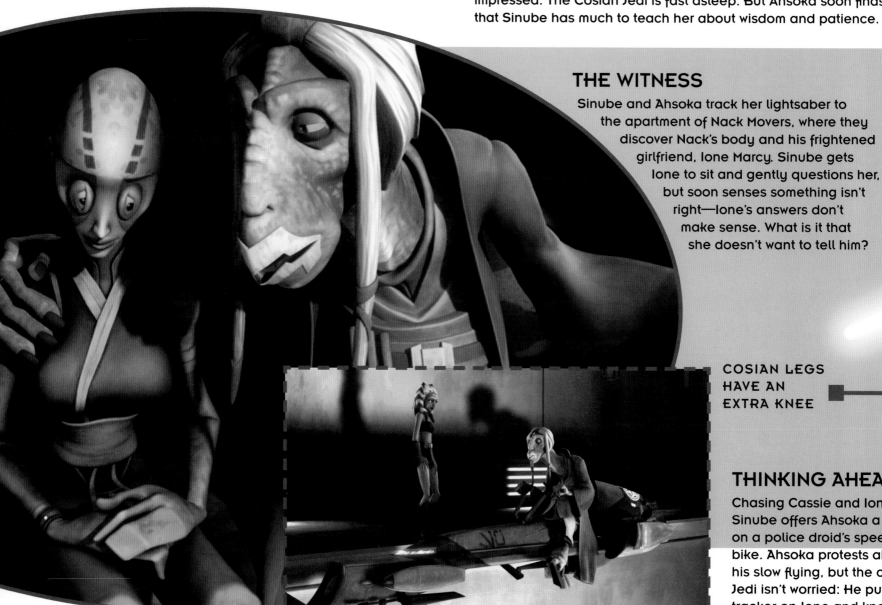

THE WITNESS

Sinube and Ahsoka track her lightsaber to the apartment of Nack Movers, where they discover Nack's body and his frightened girlfriend, Ione Marcy. Sinube gets Ione to sit and gently questions her, but soon senses something isn't right—Ione's answers don't make sense. What is it that she doesn't want to tell him?

COSIAN LEGS HAVE AN EXTRA KNEE

THINKING AHEAD

Chasing Cassie and Ione, Sinube offers Ahsoka a ride on a police droid's speeder bike. Ahsoka protests about his slow flying, but the old Jedi isn't worried: He put a tracker on Ione and knows exactly where she's going.

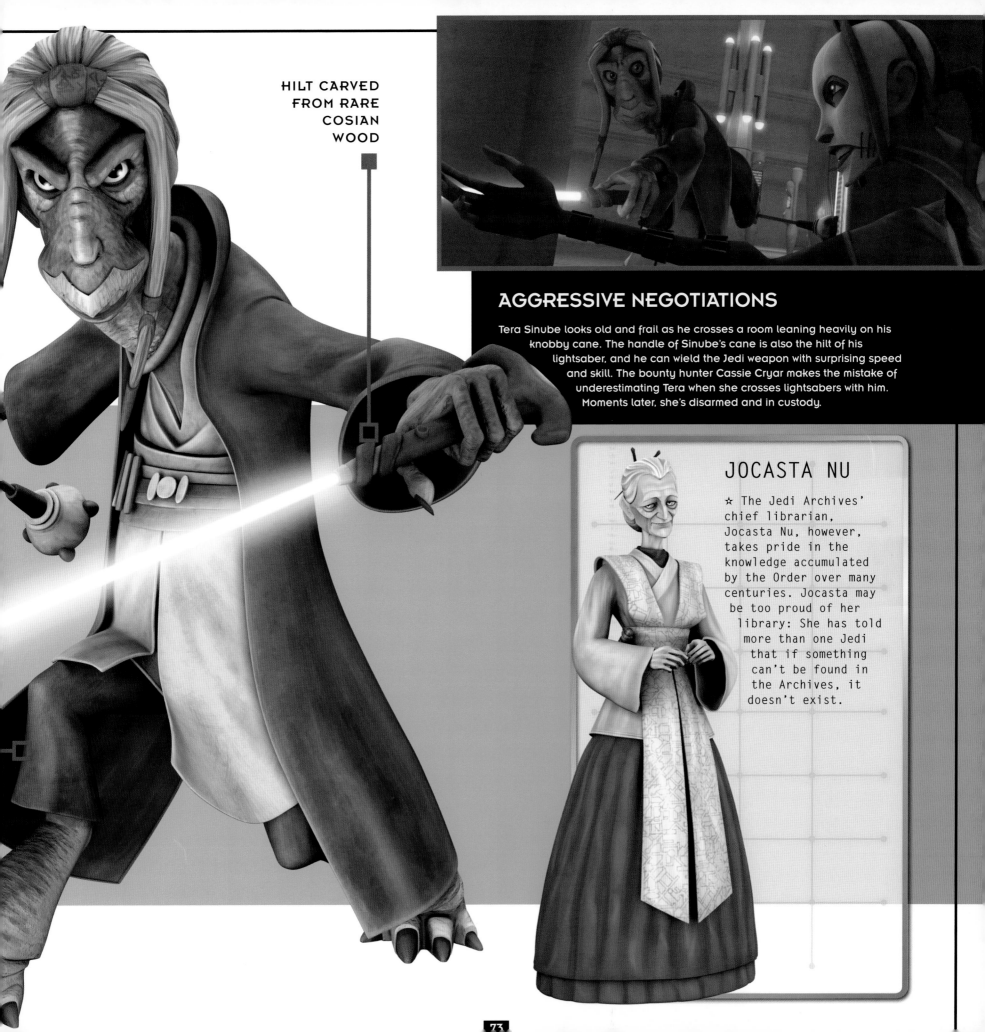

HILT CARVED FROM RARE COSIAN WOOD

AGGRESSIVE NEGOTIATIONS

Tera Sinube looks old and frail as he crosses a room leaning heavily on his knobby cane. The handle of Sinube's cane is also the hilt of his lightsaber, and he can wield the Jedi weapon with surprising speed and skill. The bounty hunter Cassie Cryar makes the mistake of underestimating Tera when she crosses lightsabers with him. Moments later, she's disarmed and in custody.

JOCASTA NU

☆ The Jedi Archives' chief librarian, Jocasta Nu, however, takes pride in the knowledge accumulated by the Order over many centuries. Jocasta may be too proud of her library: She has told more than one Jedi that if something can't be found in the Archives, it doesn't exist.

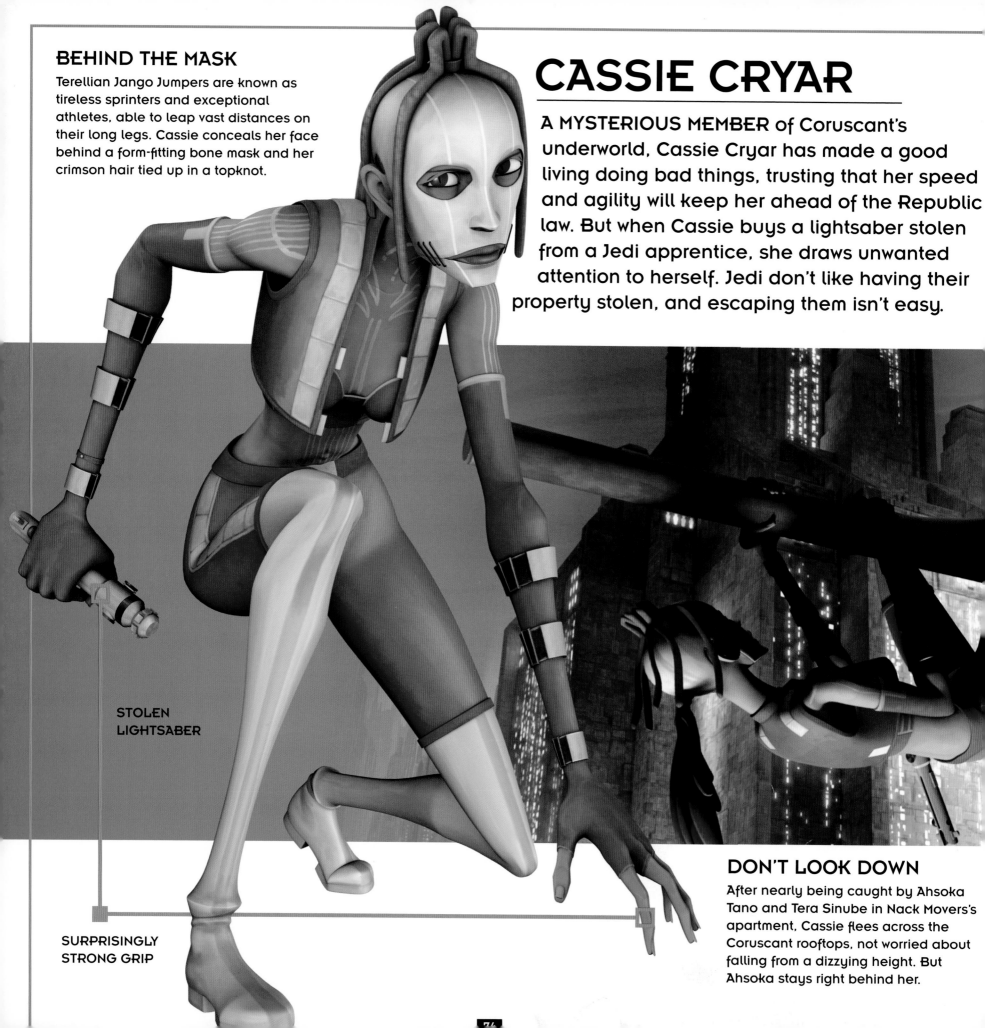

BEHIND THE MASK

Terellian Jango Jumpers are known as tireless sprinters and exceptional athletes, able to leap vast distances on their long legs. Cassie conceals her face behind a form-fitting bone mask and her crimson hair tied up in a topknot.

CASSIE CRYAR

A MYSTERIOUS MEMBER of Coruscant's underworld, Cassie Cryar has made a good living doing bad things, trusting that her speed and agility will keep her ahead of the Republic law. But when Cassie buys a lightsaber stolen from a Jedi apprentice, she draws unwanted attention to herself. Jedi don't like having their property stolen, and escaping them isn't easy.

STOLEN LIGHTSABER

SURPRISINGLY STRONG GRIP

DON'T LOOK DOWN

After nearly being caught by Ahsoka Tano and Tera Sinube in Nack Movers's apartment, Cassie flees across the Coruscant rooftops, not worried about falling from a dizzying height. But Ahsoka stays right behind her.

SHOWDOWN

Cassie imagines her new lightsaber will make her equal to a Jedi. But using the weapon of a Jedi doesn't make you a member of the Order. Tera Sinube looks old and slow, but Cassie is no match for his years of skill and experience.

THE GETAWAY

It's easy to blend into the crowd when you live on a planet that's one enormous city. Cassie and Ione flee to one of Coruscant's hover-train stations, hoping to beat the Jedi and the police there and lose themselves among busy travelers of many species.

IONE MERCY

☆ Nack Movers's girlfriend tells the Jedi that a bunch of men killed the Trandoshan. Young Ione Marcy seems terrified, but her story doesn't seem to add up. Tera Sinube has seen his share of witnesses and crime scenes, and everything he knows tells him that Ione isn't being honest. When the police droids arrive, Ione leaps out the window and flees.

FUSED FINGERS ON HAND

NACK MOVERS

The pickpocket Bannamu tells Ahsoka and Tera Sinube that he sold her lightsaber to Nack Movers, a shady Trandoshan who lives with his girlfriend in a neighborhood called Happyland. When Ahsoka and Tera find Nack's apartment, the scene is anything but happy: It sure doesn't look like Nack is going to be answering any of their questions.

2 Igniting Ahsoka's lightsaber, Cassie cuts through several billboards floating above the city.

5 Ahsoka chases Cassie across a perilously narrow pipe. Don't look down!

1 Fleeing the scene of Nack Movers's death, Terellian Jango Jumper Cassie Cryar leaps across the rooftops of Coruscant, still in possession of Ahsoka's lightsaber. The Padawan uses the Force to follow, struggling to keep up with the acrobatic Cassie's speed and jumping ability.

3 The wrecked signs begin to sink, forcing Ahsoka to make a desperate leap to avoid what would be a fatal fall.

4 Sliding down the face of a sinking billboard, Ahsoka looks for a way to continue her pursuit of Cassie.

escapes Ahsoka in arcy's speeder, but Tera ows her destination.

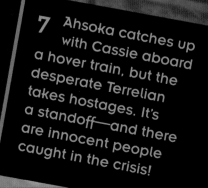

7 Ahsoka catches up with Cassie aboard a hover train, but the desperate Terrelian takes hostages. It's a standoff—and there are innocent people caught in the crisis!

DUCHESS SATINE

THE LEADER of Mandalore, Duchess Satine Kryze is a passionate voice for peace in the galaxy, speaking out against the war as head of the Council of Neutral Systems. Satine knows that her people will always be viewed with suspicion because of their warrior past, but is convinced that Mandalore can teach others the value of rejecting war as an abomination against the values of all civilized worlds.

ELABORATE HEADDRESS

KALEVALAN HAIRSTYLE

UNEASY PEACE

Some Mandalorians disagree with Satine's ideas, wishing to return the planet to its warlike ways. Satine knows her life is in constant danger, but refuses to back down from what she believes.

MANDALORE

An ancient war with the Jedi turned parts of Mandalore into deserts of white sand. Now, marvelous cube cities are home to Mandalorians who have rejected the old ways and used their gifts as inventors and builders to create a new civilization.

CASUAL CLOTHES FOR TRAVELING

OLD TIES

★ Obi-Wan Kenobi is frustrated by Satine's stubbornness, but can't hide his affection for her. Years ago he and Qui-Gon Jinn kept her safe during a civil war, and they grew close while on the run from her enemies. Obi-Wan and the Duchess find their feelings for each other remain strong.

THE PRIME MINISTER

Prime Minister Almec is one of Satine's closest allies, and a champion of Mandalore's new traditions. A proud diplomat, he dismisses the threats to Satine's rule as the work of a few radicals, and is angered by Obi-Wan's questions about Jango Fett—a man he dismisses as a mere bounty hunter wearing stolen armor.

SATINE'S GUARDS

Satine's Mandalorian Guards wear armor that recalls her planet's traditions, but they are trained for discipline and restraint in keeping her safe. But they will fight when they must, and they join the Republic's clone troopers to defend Satine's ship, the *Coronet*, when squads of Super Battle Droids attack the vessel.

MANDALORIANS

MANDALORIANS WERE ONCE nomads who fought in many wars as mercenaries. The members of the Death Watch movement disagree with Duchess Satine's pacifism and the New Mandalorians' love of advanced technology, seeing both as a betrayal of their ancient clan traditions. The Death Watch is led in secret by Pre Vizsla, who has risen to become the governor of the moon Concordia.

TRUSTED ALLY

Satine sees Vizsla as a friend and ally in her fight against the Death Watch. She has no idea that the governor is actually one of her sworn enemies who thinks her beliefs have made the Mandalorian name the subject of mockery.

SECRET MASTER

In reality, Vizsla is taking orders from Count Dooku, the leader of the Separatists. With Dooku's help, Vizsla hopes to overthrow Satine and restore the honor his planet lost long ago.

GRIM DISCOVERY

Centuries ago, ugly mines scarred Concordia's surface, worked by miners seeking beskar, the legendary Mandalorian iron. Now the mines are quiet and the warriors have died out. Or so Obi-Wan believes until he finds the mines are active again—and Pre Vizsla is not whom he appears to be.

TRADITIONAL ARMOR

UNMASKED

After Satine races off to find Obi-Wan, Vizsla realizes Death Watch's secret is out and he can no longer keep his own. So he summons his warriors, dons his traditional armor and prepares for the fight he's wanted for so many years.

NO MERCY

Death Watch hasn't grown strong by tolerating failure, as one unfortunate warrior discovers when Vizsla arrives at the group's secret mining camp.

BLACK BLADE

Among Pre Vizsla's secrets: He is the owner of an ancient weapon called the Darksaber. Vizsla claims his ancestors stole it from the Jedi Temple and used it to kill many Jedi. If Obi-Wan isn't careful, he will be another casualty.

CLAN VIZSLA

The Vizslas are an ancient Mandalorian clan whose members have included bounty hunters, warlords and Death Watch leaders, as well as peace-loving New Mandalorians. Pre dreams of making the name feared again.

ANCIENT DARKSABER

1 Concordia's mines are active once more, turning out Mandalorian helmets and armor. But before Obi-Wan can tell Duchess Satine what he has found, he's attacked and captured by the Death Watch!

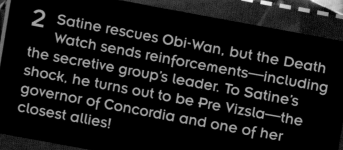

2 Satine rescues Obi-Wan, but the Death Watch sends reinforcements—including the secretive group's leader. To Satine's shock, he turns out to be Pre Vizsla—the governor of Concordia and one of her closest allies!

"WE'LL HAVE TO STAND AND FIGHT."

3 Vizsla tosses Obi-Wan his lightsaber and draws his own weapon—an ancient energy blade he claims has taken the lives of many Jedi Knights!

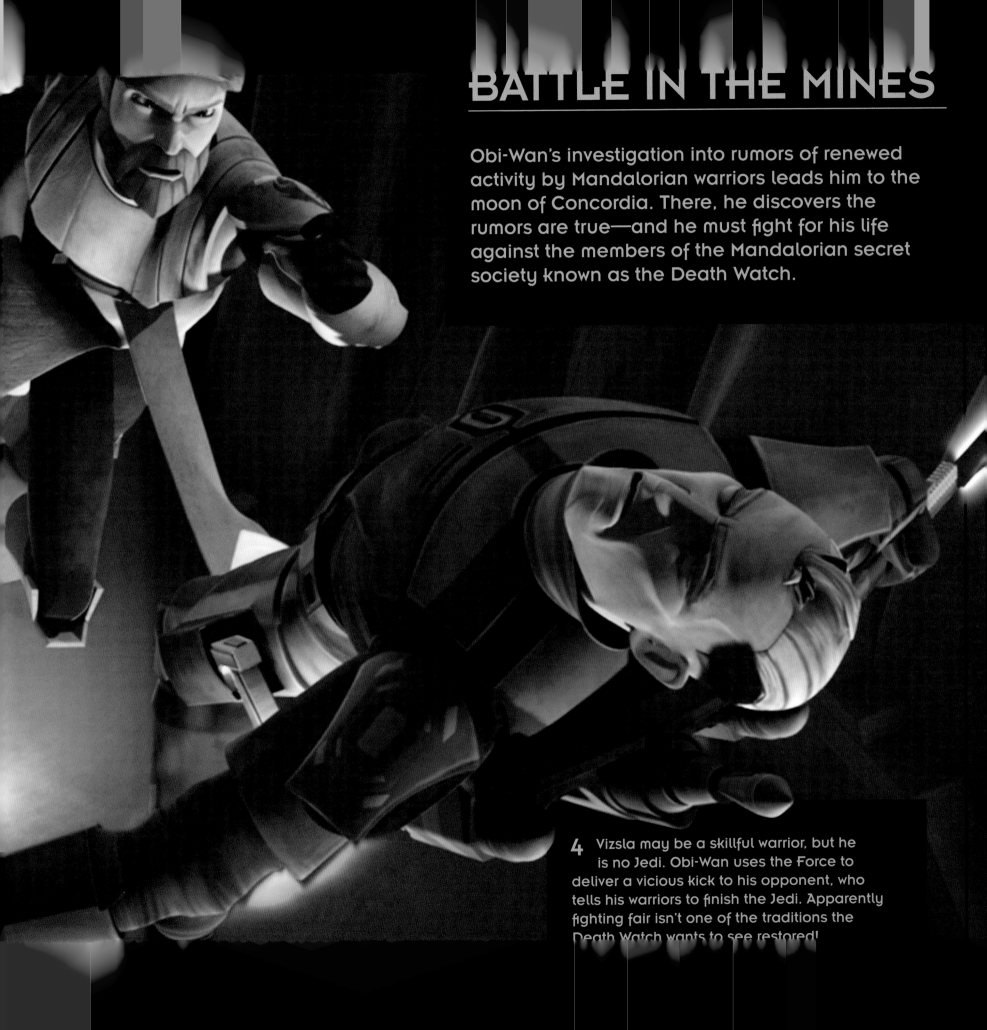

BATTLE IN THE MINES

Obi-Wan's investigation into rumors of renewed activity by Mandalorian warriors leads him to the moon of Concordia. There, he discovers the rumors are true—and he must fight for his life against the members of the Mandalorian secret society known as the Death Watch.

4 Vizsla may be a skillful warrior, but he is no Jedi. Obi-Wan uses the Force to deliver a vicious kick to his opponent, who tells his warriors to finish the Jedi. Apparently fighting fair isn't one of the traditions the Death Watch wants to see restored!

THE *CORONET*

DUCHESS SATINE and four Senator guests travel aboard her luxury starship, the *Coronet*. Satine hopes to persuade Republic loyalists Orn Free Taa and Onaconda Farr to join the Council of Neutral Systems. But someone has smuggled assassin droids aboard the ship. Which of her guests is the traitor?

THE SHIP

★ Shipwrights from Satine's homeworld of Kalevala designed and built the *Coronet*, one of the grandest luxury liners of the age. The ship's passengers travel in comfort and security, protected by a thick hull and navigation programs alert for any danger.

DEEP SPACE MYSTERY

Someone smuggled assassin droids aboard in a crate with a Senatorial seal. But who? Orn Free Taa or Onaconda Farr, who swear loyalty to the Republic? Or Kin Robb or Tal Merrik, both Satine's allies?

ORN FREE TAA

A Twi'lek Senator known for his great appetite and reputation for corruption, Orn Free Taa has been a dedicated supporter of Chancellor Palpatine. In fact, Satine wondered why he would even consider her arguments for pacifism. But Taa is also famously terrified at the mere thought of assassin droids.

KIN ROBB

Kin Robb represents Taris, a faded city-world uncomfortably close to the front lines of the civil war now tearing apart the galaxy. She fears Separatist attack and has allied herself with Satine in hopes that the war will bypass her planet, which makes her an unlikely traitor.

**DEEP-FRIED
NUNA LEGS**

**AN EXPENSIVE
KALEVALAN WINE**

**FLATWARE MADE
OF BESKAR IRON**

TAL MERRIK

Kalevala's Senator, Tal Merrik, has been a friend and ally of Duchess Satine's for years, helping recruit new worlds to the Council of Neutral Systems. Merrik seems to hate not just war but conflict of any kind, often calming arguments with gentle words. If he's a traitor, who can Satine trust?

ONACONDA FARR

Onaconda Farr represents Rodia and he did betray Padmé Amidala to Nute Gunray. But Farr was desperate to find help for his starving world and has apologized publicly for what he says was a terrible mistake. Could he have made another one?

A TRAITOR REVEALED

1 Once aboard the *Coronet*, the assassin droids release hordes of tiny, deadly probes that swarm over anyone in their path.

2 A captured probe refuses to attack Merrik, revealing his guilt. But the treasonous Senator takes Satine hostage, holding her at gunpoint and taunting Obi-Wan.

Tal Merrik takes Duchess Satine hostage, hoping to drag her off as a prisoner of the Separatists. Obi-Wan is helpless to free the woman he loves—but Anakin rushes to the rescue!

3 Merrik asks Obi-Wan if he can strike him down in cold blood and make a mockery of Satine's ideals. Obi-Wan isn't sure what to do—but Anakin doesn't hesitate.

"COME ON, THEN. WHO WILL STRIKE FIRST?"

DAVU GOLEC

DAVU GOLEC NEVER wanted to be a hero: He's a bureaucrat with the Republic Ministry of Intelligence, where he monitors intercepted transmissions to aid the war effort. When he discovers someone has edited a Mandalorian transmission to change its meaning, he realizes maybe only he can prevent a war.

MINISTRY RANK BADGE

UNALTERED COPY OF RECORDING

HOPES FOR PEACE

Golec doesn't know who is faking evidence for war with Mandalore, but hopes Satine can bring the truth to the Senate.

A SECRET MEETING

A tape played for the Senate seems to show Mandalorian officials asking for Republic intervention. But Golec finds the unaltered tape, and it says something else entirely. He copies the tape onto a recording disc and brings it to Duchess Satine.

FIGHTING A LIE

Golec knows truth is often the first casualty in war, but he's horrified to learn someone in the government he serves is faking evidence, and he makes up his mind to stop them.

STOPPING THE TRUTH

When Davu Golec meets with Duchess Satine, he has no idea that a Death Watch assassin has him in his sights. The group will not let Golec stand in the way of their plan for a Republic invasion of Mandalore.

TOUGH
PLASTOID
RIOT SHIELD

STUN BATON FOR
CROWD CONTROL

RIOT TROOPERS

Special squads of clone troopers are trained for crowd control on Coruscant and other worlds. These troops are taught to keep order while using the minimum amount of force.

PHOTO RECEPTORS
SEE IN INFRAREDN

POLICE

☆ Police droids are common sights on Coruscant's lower levels, where they use their keen sensors to watch for crime and hunt fugitives. They carry stun batons and can call on riot troopers for backup when a situation becomes too dangerous.

PLOT AGAINST MANDALORE

1 Duchess Satine is lucky to escape alive when a Death Watch assassin blows up her airspeeder. The Republic calls it an accident, but Satine knows better!

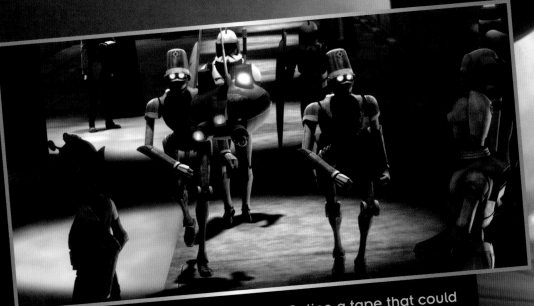

2 Davu Golec gives Satine a tape that could avert the war, but is shot by an assassin. Police droids blame Satine and hunt her through Coruscant's seedy lower levels.

Someone wants a war between Mandalore and the Republic—and they're willing to kill to make it happen.

3 After Obi-Wan takes the tape and promises to deliver it to Padmé Amidala, Satine allows herself to be captured by Senate guards.

"YOU WERE RIGHT—SOMEONE FAKED THE EVIDENCE."

4 As Republic warships prepare to head to Mandalore, Padmé plays the tape for the Senate, revealing that the evidence was faked. There will be no war!

LOLO PURS

AS A RODIAN Representative, Lolo Purs's job is to assist Onaconda Farr with the planet's legislative affairs, which includes rounding up votes that would halt production of more clones. She is outspoken on behalf of her planet and friends, who repeatedly urge her to keep control of her emotions.

TAKEN INTO CUSTODY

After she's revealed as Farr's killer, Lolo tries to make her getaway by taking Padmé Amidala hostage. But Padmé only seems fragile—one well-aimed punch knocks Lolo out cold.

HE WAS MY MENTOR

After Onaconda's sudden death, Lolo appears overcome with sorrow. Senator Farr was her mentor, and she doesn't know how she will go on without him. At Farr's funeral, Padmé tries to comfort her, but Palpatine's guards interrupt them. Coruscant's police think Farr didn't die of natural causes, but that he was murdered!

EYES CAN SEE IN INFRARED

HOLD-OUT PISTOL

RODIAN REVENGE

Padmé long ago forgave her Uncle Ono for betraying her, but Lolo has been unable to do the same. She remains enraged by the weakness that Farr showed, and is convinced that Rodia needs a strong Senator to make the case for galactic peace.

UMBARAN SILK TUNIC

POLISHED WALKING CANE

HALLE & CO.

☆ The bill sought by Farr and his friends is opposed by Halle Burtoni, the Senator from Kamino, and her ally, Umbara's Mee Deechi. As the center of clone production, Kamino has grown rich during the war, and Burtoni seeks to keep the credits flowing. Deechi is a fiery supporter of the war, and tells Padmé that trying to end the fighting is unpatriotic.

ONACONDA'S MISTAKE

When a blockaded Rodia was starving, a desperate Farr made a short-lived bargain with the Separatists, handing Padmé over to them in exchange for food and medicine. Farr's betrayal of his old friend has haunted him ever since, and he has worked tirelessly to end the war.

SENATORIAL CUMMERBUND

FORMAL GOWN OF RICH FABRIC

POLITICAL POISON

Lolo slips a Kaminoan-made poison that affects only Rodians into the wine. After Padmé's speech, Lolo, Farr, Padmé, Bail Organa, and Mon Mothma sip the wine. Even if the poison were found, no one would suspect Lolo as the culprit. But she forgets to pretend to drink—a detail that doesn't escape Padmé's notice.

BAIL ORGANA

THE SENATOR FROM ALDERAAN, Bail Organa is respected for a sense of fairness and a passion for justice. He is a strong supporter of the Republic, but firm in his belief that you can be patriotic while still questioning the war with the Separatists. He worries about growing militarism among the citizens of the galaxy.

DIRECT APPROACH

Bail thinks of the Senate Building as his arena, but his growing friendship with the apparently fearless Senator Padmé Amidala has led him to places he never imagined being—such as Coruscant's seedy dockside district.

THE PEACE MOVEMENT

Organa has become a leader of the Republic's peace movement, backing legislation to reduce military spending and to stop production of new clone armies. Together with Padmé, Mon Mothma, and Onaconda Farr, he seeks other Senators' support.

TRAPPED!

Bail's mission to the strategic world of Christophsis turns dangerous when an armada of Separatist warships led by Admiral Trench attack the planet. Republic forces rush to the scene: Christophsis sits on a key trade route into the Outer Rim, and a Senator as important as Organa would make a valuable hostage for Count Dooku. Trapped on the surface, Bail can only wonder if a rescue will come in time.

A FRIEND'S SECRETS

Politicians are shrewd judges of character, and Bail senses that Padmé Amidala is more than just friends with the dashing Jedi Anakin Skywalker. But Bail is also a diplomat, so he never asks the Senator from Naboo about the nature of their relationship.

ALDERAAN

Alderaan is a Core World celebrated for its arts and dedication to peace. It was one of the first planets to join the Republic thousands of years ago.

MON MOTHMA

★ The Senator from Chandrila, Mon Mothma is a friend of Bail and a mentor to Padmé Amidala. Mon is determined to seek a peaceful solution to the war tearing apart the galaxy. She has led the legislative fight to reduce military budgets despite the efforts of Senators such as Kamino's Halle Burtoni and her ally Mee Deechi.

TEAM DIVO

Divo travels with a squad of police droids for backup—and never makes a move without his trusty valet droid LEP-171B. 171B keeps track of Divo's many datapads, passing them to his master as needed.

TAN DIVO

TAN DIVO IS A lieutenant in the police department responsible for Coruscant's Senate District. A veteran inspector, Divo has seen many crimes in his day—too many to think that politicians and elected officials aren't capable of murder. Divo hates crime: It's messy, leads to lots of paperwork, and is against the rules. Murder? That's particularly bad—and not just for whoever it is who gets killed. Do you know how many reports are generated by one murder?

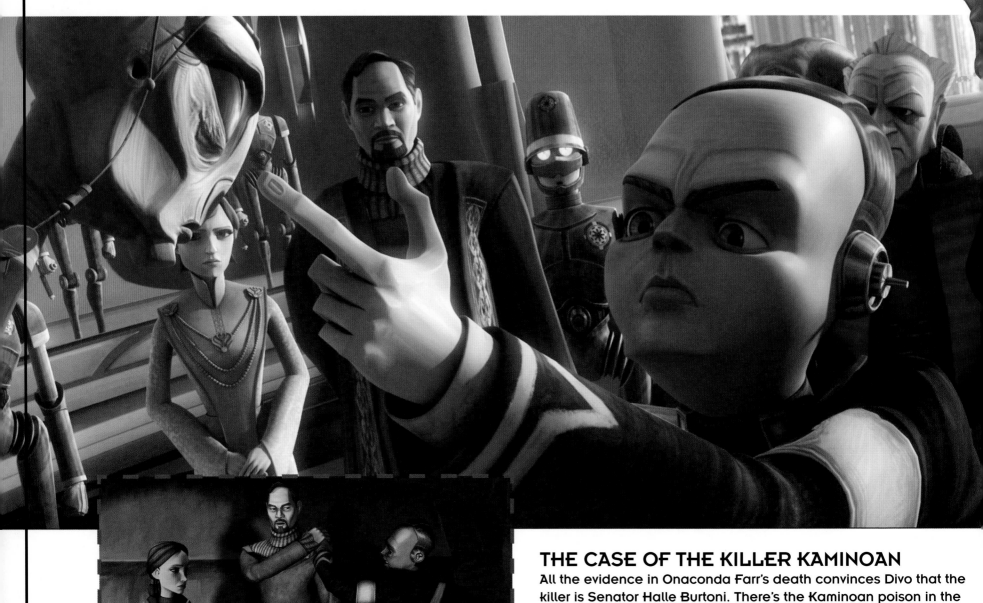

THE CASE OF THE KILLER KAMINOAN

All the evidence in Onaconda Farr's death convinces Divo that the killer is Senator Halle Burtoni. There's the Kaminoan poison in the glass, the attempt to kill Senators Organa and Amidala at the docks, and the attack on Lolo Purs. Divo cuffs Burtoni—but what's Senator Amidala talking about now? This better not require another report.

COMLINK IS
ALWAYS ON

A-43
HUSHABYE
PISTOL

ONE OF MANY
DATAPADS

THERE ARE RULES

☆ Politicians! They're enough to drive a
police inspector crazy. If they're not
hiding something that will come back to
haunt them, they're disobeying police
orders and skulking around on the docks,
being shot at, and having things dropped
on them. Can't this pushy Senator Amidala
understand that she needs to care about
rules? Why, without rules life would be
chaos! Well, chaos and paperwork.

A SECRET BUSINESS

Divo figures politicians poison each other all the
time, but get away with it because they don't
have Tan Divo on the case. Senator Amidala
insists Onaconda Farr had no secrets, but Divo
isn't that naive. Politics is all about secrets!

1 Coruscant is so noisy that Padmé and Bail fail to hear the hum of a giant crane overhead—until it sends a huge container hurtling down on them!

"WHAT IF THIS WAS ALL A SETUP?"

2 Padmé chases the shadowy figure that tried to kill them, blaster in hand. But the unknown assassin is also armed—and the docks offer plenty of places to hide!

3 Jumping out of the way of tumbling containers, Bail is left hanging over a long drop. Padmé must abandon her pursuit of the killer to save her friend!

AMBUSH AT THE DOCKS

After learning that Onaconda Farr had a mysterious meeting at the Coruscant docks before his death, Padmé and Bail Organa search the dockyard for clues—unaware that an assassin lurks in the shadows!

ADMIRAL TRENCH

A HARCH FROM SECUNDUS ANDO, Admiral Trench was a feared commander for the Corporate Alliance in the years before the Clone Wars. He was believed killed during the Battle of Malastare Narrows, but somehow survived and now leads a flotilla of Separatist warships above the besieged planet Christophsis. That's bad news for the Republic: Trench is a master of military tactics and relentless when he discovers an opponent's weaknesses.

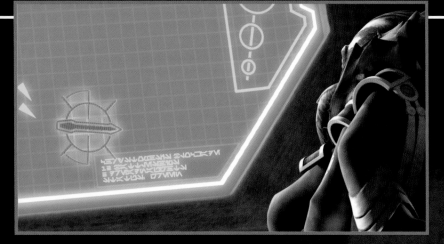

A SECRET REVEALED

Anakin fires torpedoes at Trench to draw his attention away from the Republic personnel trapped on Christophsis. But now the admiral knows there's a stealth ship in the area.

BATTLE DROID ACTING AS PILOT

EYES ARE SENSITIVE TO MOVEMENT AND LIGHT

CHELICERAE EVOLVED TO HOLD PREY IN PLACE

HELLO UGLY

Trench hasn't had a worthy opponent in a long time and can't resist toying with his prey by contacting the pilot of the stealth ship.

TRENCH'S PERSONAL INSIGNIA

TEMPTING TARGET

The Separatists have targeted Christophsis because it sits on a key hyperspace route into the Outer Rim. As a bonus, their forces have trapped Bail Organa and hope to kill or capture the Senator from Alderaan.

FAMILIAR SIGNS

Watching the battle unfold above Christophsis, Admiral Yularen feels a chill run down his spine: The Separatists' tactics seem oddly familiar. Footage of the battle confirms his fears: The *Invincible* bears Trench's personal symbol.

REPUBLIC RANK BADGE

NAVAL UNIFORM

ADMIRAL YULAREN

☆ A by-the-book naval officer, Wullf Yularen serves with Anakin Skywalker, though the Jedi general's reckless habits threaten to turn his hair prematurely gray. At Christophsis, Yularen finds himself confronting an old foe he thought had perished in a long-ago battle.

CAT AND MOUSE

Trench's favorite tactic against
cloaked warships is to lock onto
their magnetic signatures with
tracking torpedos. Can Anakin
use that against the admiral?

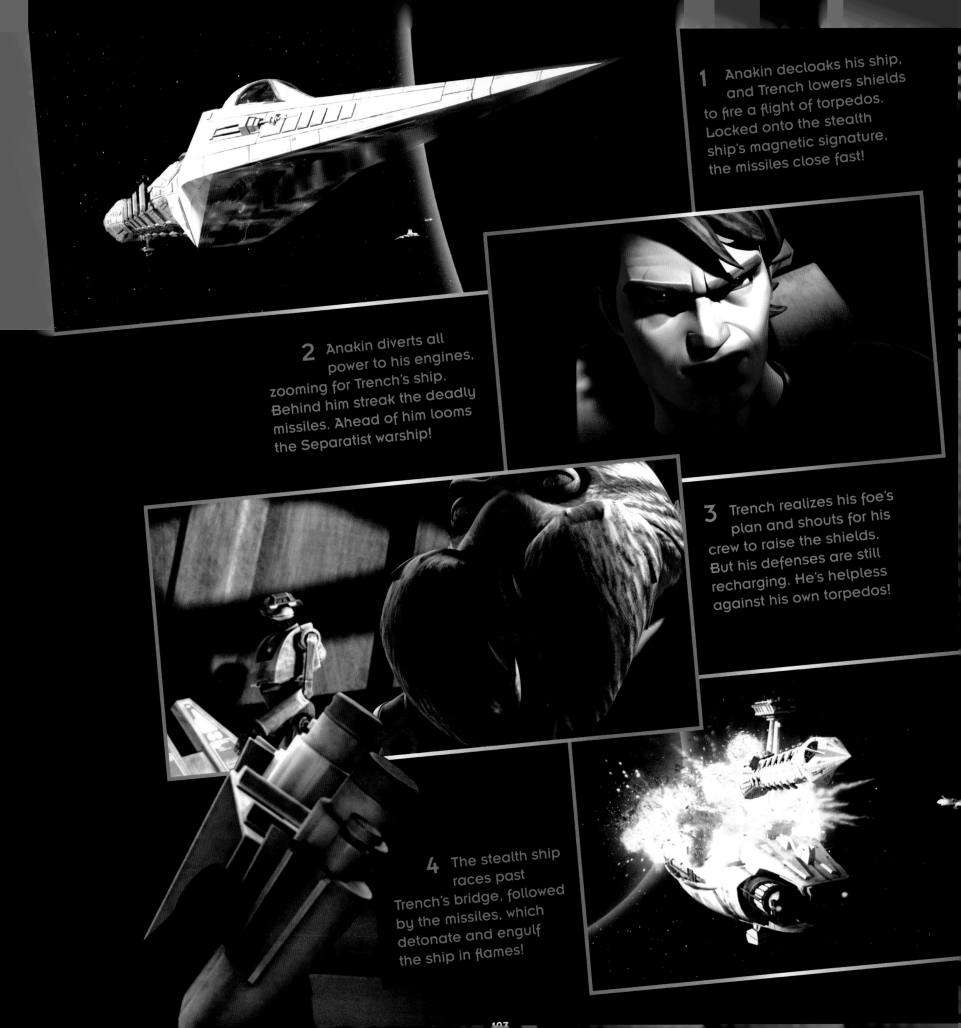

1 Anakin decloaks his ship, and Trench lowers shields to fire a flight of torpedos. Locked onto the stealth ship's magnetic signature, the missiles close fast!

2 Anakin diverts all power to his engines, zooming for Trench's ship. Behind him streak the deadly missiles. Ahead of him looms the Separatist warship!

3 Trench realizes his foe's plan and shouts for his crew to raise the shields. But his defenses are still recharging. He's helpless against his own torpedos!

4 The stealth ship races past Trench's bridge, followed by the missiles, which detonate and engulf the ship in flames!

RUMI PARAMITA

A Frenk from the planet Gorobei, Rumi offers the world a ready smile—but her brain is always sizing up situations.

AGAINST THE PIRATES

AFTER CRASH-LANDING ON Felucia, Obi-Wan, Anakin, and Ahsoka come to Akira, a village surrounded by lush fields. Pirates are threatening the villagers, who have bought protection from four mercenaries—Sugi, Embo, Rumi Paramita, and Seripas. That sounds like extortion to the Jedi, but the mercenaries have a sense of honor. They join forces. But can seven warriors defend a whole village?

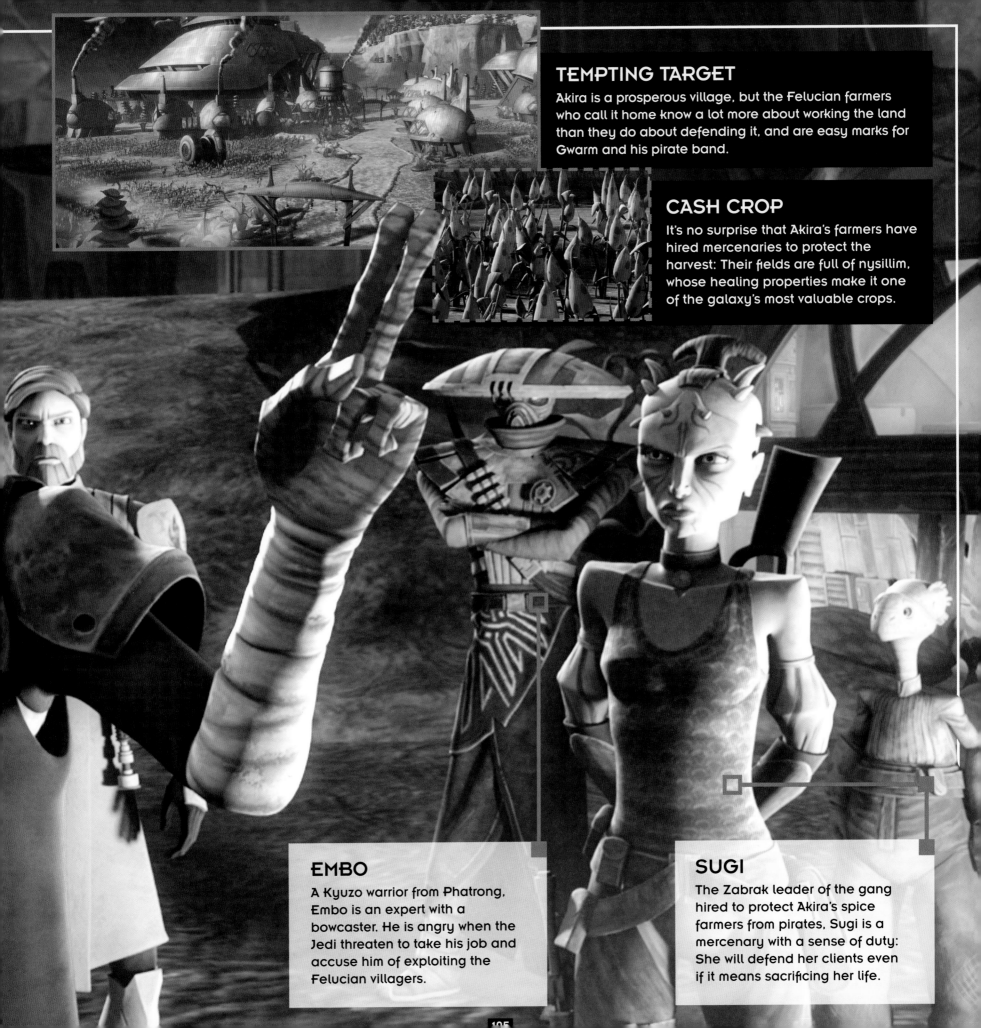

TEMPTING TARGET

Akira is a prosperous village, but the Felucian farmers who call it home know a lot more about working the land than they do about defending it, and are easy marks for Gwarm and his pirate band.

CASH CROP

It's no surprise that Akira's farmers have hired mercenaries to protect the harvest: Their fields are full of nysillim, whose healing properties make it one of the galaxy's most valuable crops.

EMBO

A Kyuzo warrior from Phatrong, Embo is an expert with a bowcaster. He is angry when the Jedi threaten to take his job and accuse him of exploiting the Felucian villagers.

SUGI

The Zabrak leader of the gang hired to protect Akira's spice farmers from pirates, Sugi is a mercenary with a sense of duty: She will defend her clients even if it means sacrificing her life.

HONDO OHNAKA

HONDO OHNAKA IS an infamous pirate of the Outer Rim. His gang's specialty is seizing ships, stealing their cargos, and ransoming the passengers, but he can't resist the prospect of raiding an entire nysillim crop—particularly with the war having driven the price of medicinal herbs to new heights.

A PLOT FOILED

Hondo's plot to sell the captive Dooku to the Republic failed when the Sith Lord escaped and the Jedi and Republic forces wrecked his gang's hideout.

WEEQUAYS

Many Weequays serve the Hutts as hired goons, and several are members of Hondo's gang. The Weequay named Gwarm tells Hondo about the rich crop on Felucia. The farmers have hired bounty hunters to defend them, but Hondo isn't concerned: Most mercenaries will switch sides if offered more credits.

COAT STOLEN
FROM CAPTURED
NOBLE

SELF-MADE MAN

Hondo's parents sold him to priests of the Weequay god Quay, but he escaped by stowing away on a ship to the Hutt world of Boonta. There, he became a trusted servant of the crime lord Porla the Hutt, but then ran away from Porla to begin a life of piracy.

GOGGLES FAVORED
BY SWOOP RIDERS

THE EQUALIZER

When he led the escape from Porla's service, Hondo helped himself to weapons and other gear that belonged to the Hutt, including several powerful Ubrikkian tanks. As Hondo likes to say, negotiations tend to go better when you speak softly... and drive a big tank.

PILF MUKMUK IS
A FAVORITE PET

PIRATE PETS

☆ Hondo has learned that it is an absurd galaxy, and the best thing you can do is laugh at whatever fate has in store for you. The pirate keeps Kowakian monkey lizards as pets, because he loves their habit of laughing out loud when it's least appropriate.

READY FOR ACTION

Hondo has already seen one good plan wrecked by the interference of the Jedi, and it's an experience he'd rather not go through again. Just in case, Hondo has acquired an electrostaff—the feared weapon of Dooku's MagnaGuards. The shafts of electrostaffs are made out of phrik, an alloy too strong to be severed by the slash of a Jedi's lightsaber.

SERIPAS

SERIPAS IS AN INTIMIDATING sight—a hulking warrior whose steel limbs bristle with weapons. But as Ahsoka discovers on Felucia, Seripas is less than meets the eye. That armor hides a skinny creature not even a a meter tall. Still, as Ahsoka points out, you don't have to look tough to be tough.

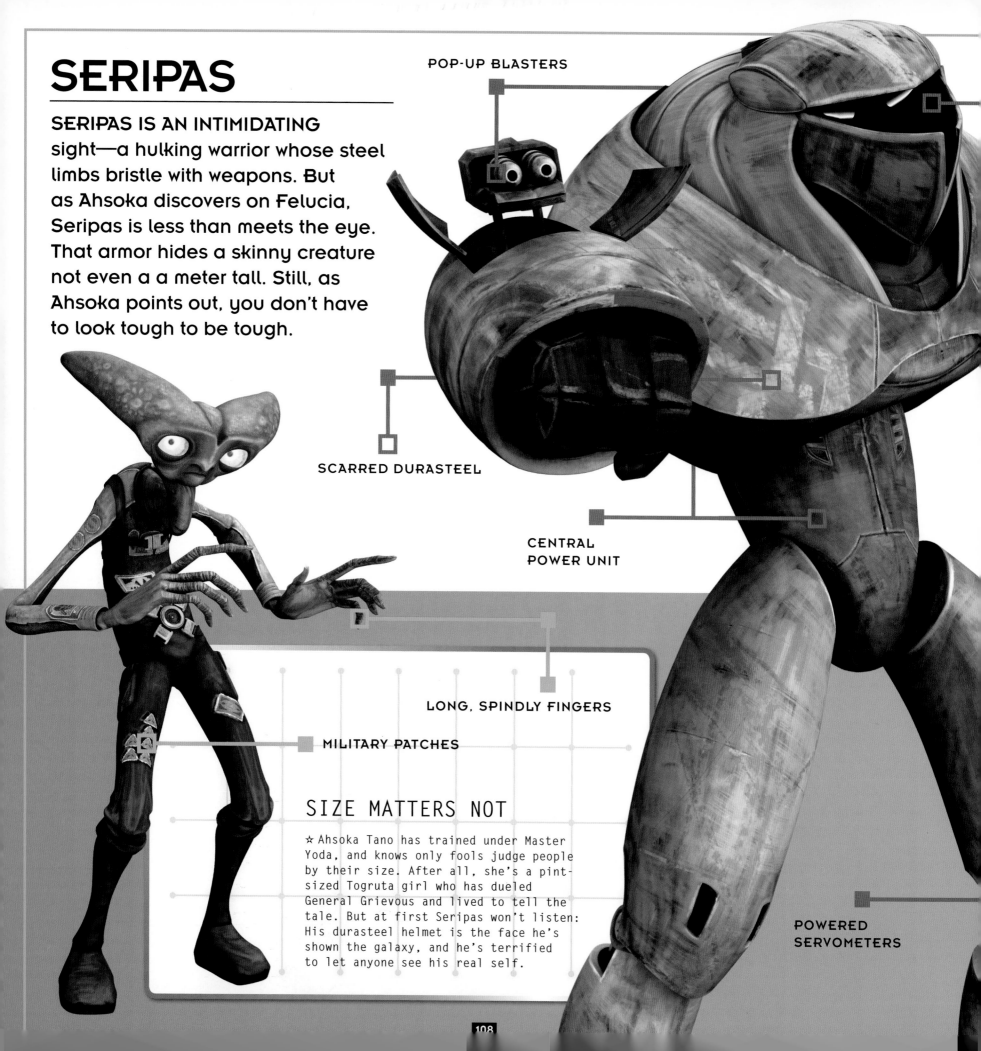

POP-UP BLASTERS

SCARRED DURASTEEL

CENTRAL POWER UNIT

LONG, SPINDLY FINGERS

MILITARY PATCHES

POWERED SERVOMETERS

SIZE MATTERS NOT

☆ Ahsoka Tano has trained under Master Yoda, and knows only fools judge people by their size. After all, she's a pint-sized Togruta girl who has dueled General Grievous and lived to tell the tale. But at first Seripas won't listen: His durasteel helmet is the face he's shown the galaxy, and he's terrified to let anyone see his real self.

HELMET HIDES EYES

POWERED GAUNTLETS

POWERED ARMOR

Powered suits of armor like Seripas's can make a soldier into a one-man assault vehicle. But such armor is expensive and difficult to operate, which limits its effectiveness in combat. Given that, exoskeletons like Seripas's are rare.

FOUR AGAINST ONE... OR TWO

The Jedi's first meeting with Seripas and his fellow mercenaries isn't friendly: Anakin and Ahsoka square off against the four hunters, sabers and blasters raised. When Rumi notes that four against one isn't a fair fight, Ahsoka objects: What about her? "We don't count you, knee-high," rumbles Seripas.

SUIT MALFUNCTION

As Akira's villagers prepare for battle, a misfired stone and a felled tree leave Seripas lying on the ground, helmet knocked off. As Anakin's Padawan looks on in shock, a tiny alien head pops out and squeaks at Ahsoka not to look—he's having a suit malfunction! Seripas's secret is out!

ON HIS OWN

Battling the pirate band, Seripas finds that his bulky armor leaves him too slow to hit pirates whizzing by on speeder bikes. He gets up his courage, opens his suit, and leaps nimbly onto the back of a passing pirate.

1 Akira's villagers fight Gwarm and his fellow thugs man-to-man, showing that they've learned to defend themselves. But their bravery will be wasted if Anakin can't take out Hondo Ohnaka's tank!

"YOUR SITUATION IS HOPELESS SKYWALKER!"

2 The Jedi and the Weequay pirate exchange blows atop the lurching assault vehicle, with the thunder of shells drowning out the hum of Anakin's lightsaber. Anakin is an expert duelist, but Hondo fights him to a draw!

3 It's hard enough to fight on stable ground—now try it atop a moving vehicle! One false step could send either man tumbling off the speeding tank!

4 Anakin and Hondo continue their fight on the ground, and the pirate chieftain is left dangling from a cliff. Which means It's time to strike a deal: If Anakin pulls him up, Hondo will call off the attack!

BOBA FETT

BOBA FETT IS THE SON of Jango Fett, the bounty hunter whose genetic material was used to create the Republic's clone armies. In agreeing to serve as a template for Kamino's clone armies, Jango asked for an unaltered clone— Boba—who would age at a normal rate. Boba loved his father, and was horrified to see him struck down by Mace Windu in battle on Geonosis. He seeks revenge on Windu and sets a trap for him when the Jedi Master visits Admiral Kilian's flagship *Endurance*.

BOBA'S STRUGGLE

Boba wants Mace Windu to pay for what he did, but he has struggled to make himself into a ruthless killer. He is disturbed to think that his quest for revenge could kill innocents caught in the crossfire.

A CADET TO WATCH

Aboard the Endurance, Boba watches as young Jax mans a turbolaser and just misses. When Admiral Kilian gives Boba the next turn in the gunner's chair, he isn't nervous: He's spent many hours manning Slave I's guns.

YOUTH BRIGADE

☆ As a clone himself, Boba is the perfect secret agent—one no Republic officer will look at twice. The plot to kill Windu begins when he poses as Lucky, a new transfer to Sgt. Crasher's clone unit.

BELTED TUNIC IS STANDARD ISSUE

SGT. CRASHER
DOESN'T APPROVE
OF LONG HAIR

JANGO'S LEGACY

When his father died
in the Geonosis arena,
Boba inherited his ship
Slave I, his gear, and
spare weapons. Jango's
Mandalorian armor won't fit
young Boba just yet, but he is
proud to fly *Slave I* and carry
the twin pistols that were his
father's signature.

MATCHING SET OF
WESTAR-34 PISTOLS

JANGO'S UTILITY BELT
OVER SASH BINDING

FETT'S FURY

It was never Boba's plan to take hostages—he wants revenge
on Mace Windu, not credits for selling men to the Separatists.
But when Admiral Kilian tries to reach out to Boba by calling
him a good soldier, Jango's son is enraged: He's no soldier!
And don't call him a clone!

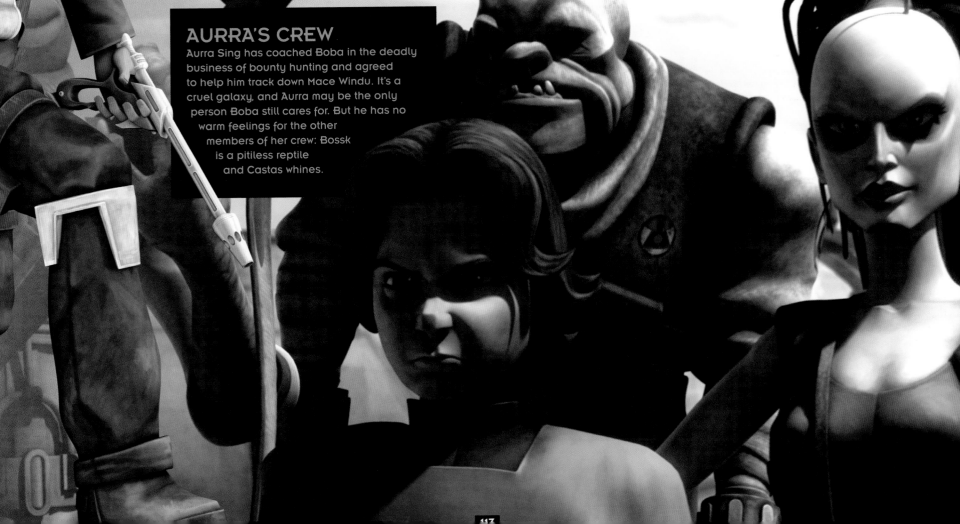

AURRA'S CREW

Aurra Sing has coached Boba in the deadly
business of bounty hunting and agreed
to help him track down Mace Windu. It's a
cruel galaxy, and Aurra may be the only
person Boba still cares for. But he has no
warm feelings for the other
members of her crew: Bossk
is a pitiless reptile
and Castas whines.

CLONE YOUTH BRIGADE

THE CLONES CREATED to serve the Republic as soldiers begin training as soon as they can walk, learning the basics of combat and military strategy and undergoing repeated tests to find good candidates for further training as pilots, gunners, and officers. In the deep space of the Outer Rim, one brigade of clone trainees gets a special assignment: the chance to tour a Republic cruiser during operations.

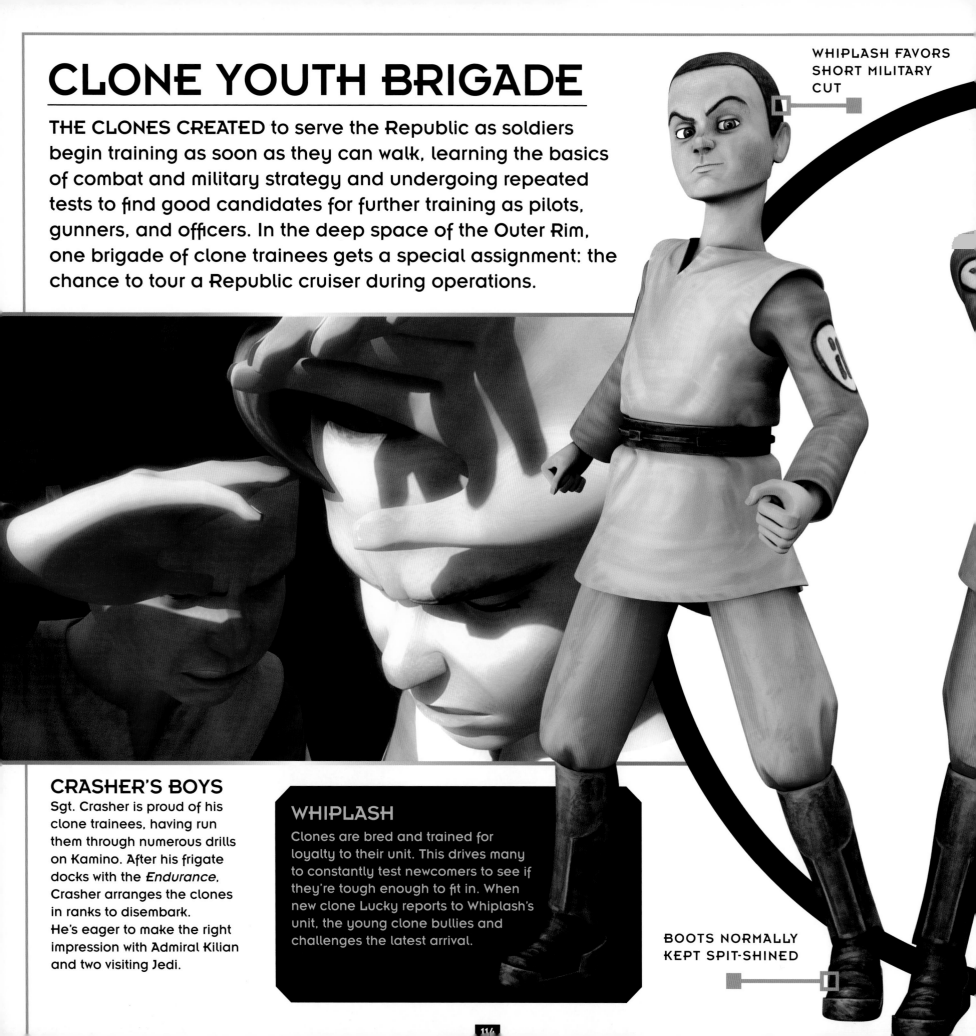

WHIPLASH FAVORS SHORT MILITARY CUT

CRASHER'S BOYS

Sgt. Crasher is proud of his clone trainees, having run them through numerous drills on Kamino. After his frigate docks with the *Endurance*, Crasher arranges the clones in ranks to disembark. He's eager to make the right impression with Admiral Kilian and two visiting Jedi.

WHIPLASH

Clones are bred and trained for loyalty to their unit. This drives many to constantly test newcomers to see if they're tough enough to fit in. When new clone Lucky reports to Whiplash's unit, the young clone bullies and challenges the latest arrival.

BOOTS NORMALLY KEPT SPIT-SHINED

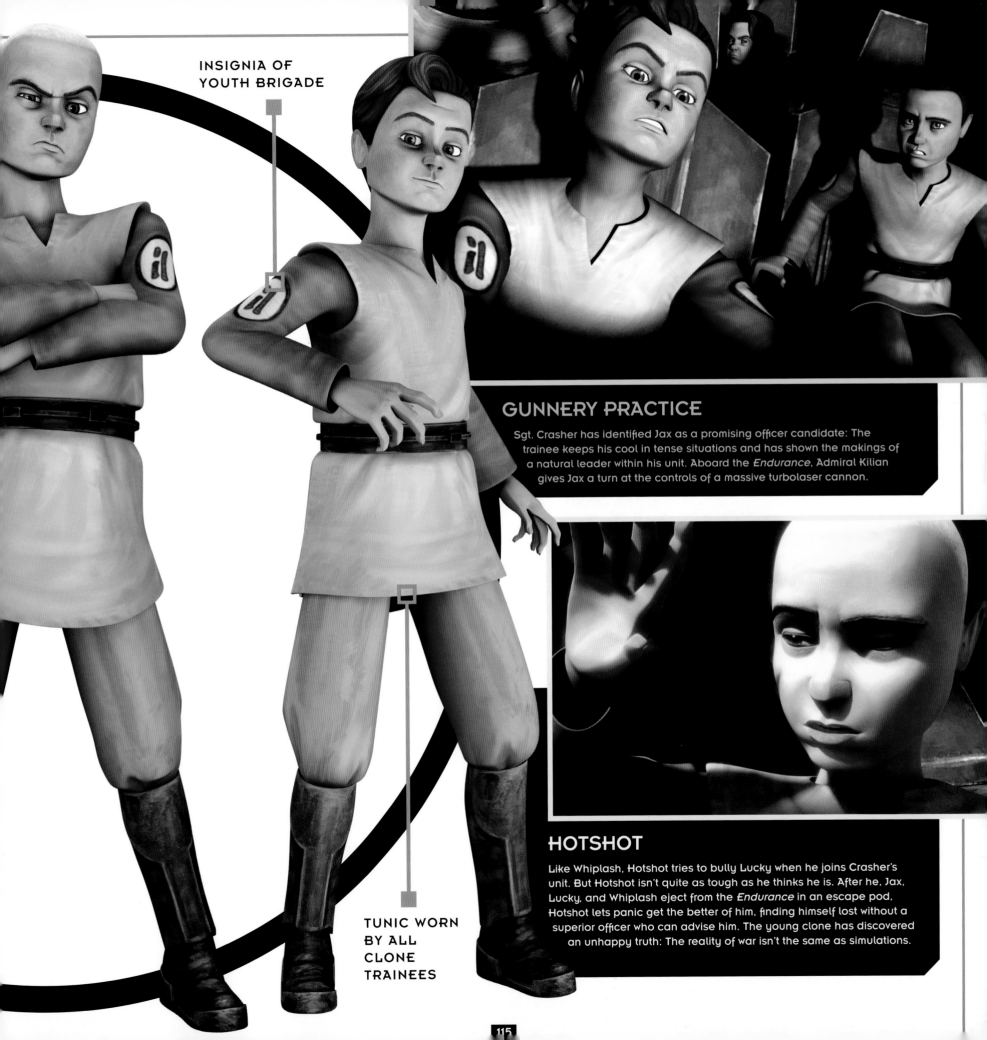

INSIGNIA OF
YOUTH BRIGADE

GUNNERY PRACTICE

Sgt. Crasher has identified Jax as a promising officer candidate: The trainee keeps his cool in tense situations and has shown the makings of a natural leader within his unit. Aboard the *Endurance*, Admiral Kilian gives Jax a turn at the controls of a massive turbolaser cannon.

HOTSHOT

Like Whiplash, Hotshot tries to bully Lucky when he joins Crasher's unit. But Hotshot isn't quite as tough as he thinks he is. After he, Jax, Lucky, and Whiplash eject from the *Endurance* in an escape pod, Hotshot lets panic get the better of him, finding himself lost without a superior officer who can advise him. The young clone has discovered an unhappy truth: The reality of war isn't the same as simulations.

TUNIC WORN
BY ALL
CLONE
TRAINEES

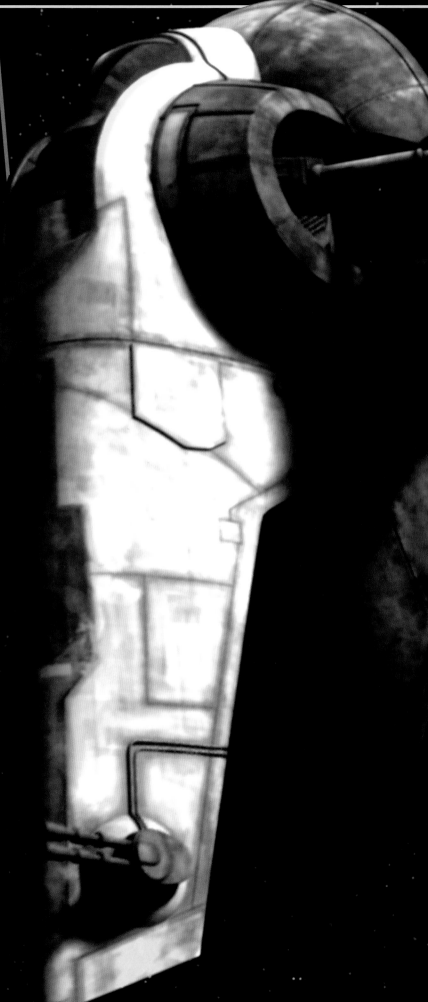

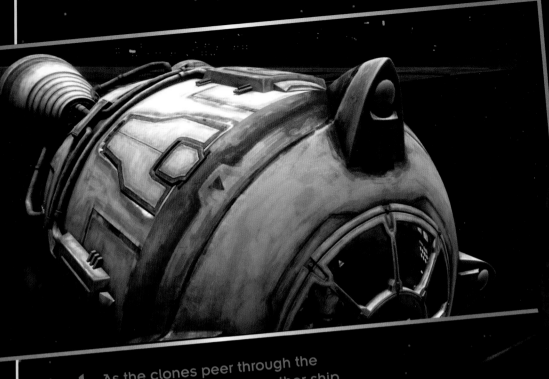

1 As the clones peer through the pod's small viewport, another ship docks with theirs. It's the battered prison ship known as *Slave I*!

2 Aurra Sing is surprised to find Boba has company. She tells him the clones have seen too much!

3 Aurra gives Boba a choice: Set the trainees adrift and come with her, or be marooned with them. What will he do?

4 Boba hardens his heart and makes his decision. He shuts the pod's hatch, and sends his friends off into deep space!

BOBA'S CHOICE

Boba Fett flees the *Endurance* along with Jax, Hotshot, and Whiplash. But as the trainees struggle to pilot their escape pod, something awaits them!

TERROR IN SPACE

Kilian and his troopers help to look for the saboteur and are nearly sucked into space when an explosion rips apart the Endurance's reactor room.

ADMIRAL KILIAN

ADMIRAL SHOAN KILIAN IS a veteran of decades of battles against pirates and slavers in the Outer Rim, and he's learned that what makes a warship effective in battle is discipline. While some of the Republic's non-clone officers dislike or resent clones, Kilian thinks their dedication and training set an excellent example for the rest of the starfleet. When Kilian's beloved Star Destroyer is attacked by a saboteur, the admiral remains cool amid the chaos and confusion.

WOUNDED WARSHIP

The blast that rips through the *Endurance*'s reactor room destroys one of the Star Destroyer's engines and disrupts her navigation systems. Her crew can do nothing to prevent a crash-landing on Vanqor.

DUTY CALLS

With the Endurance mortally wounded, Anakin and Mace urge Kilian to evacuate in one of the warship's escape pods. He refuses in a firm voice: A Republic officer stays with his ship.

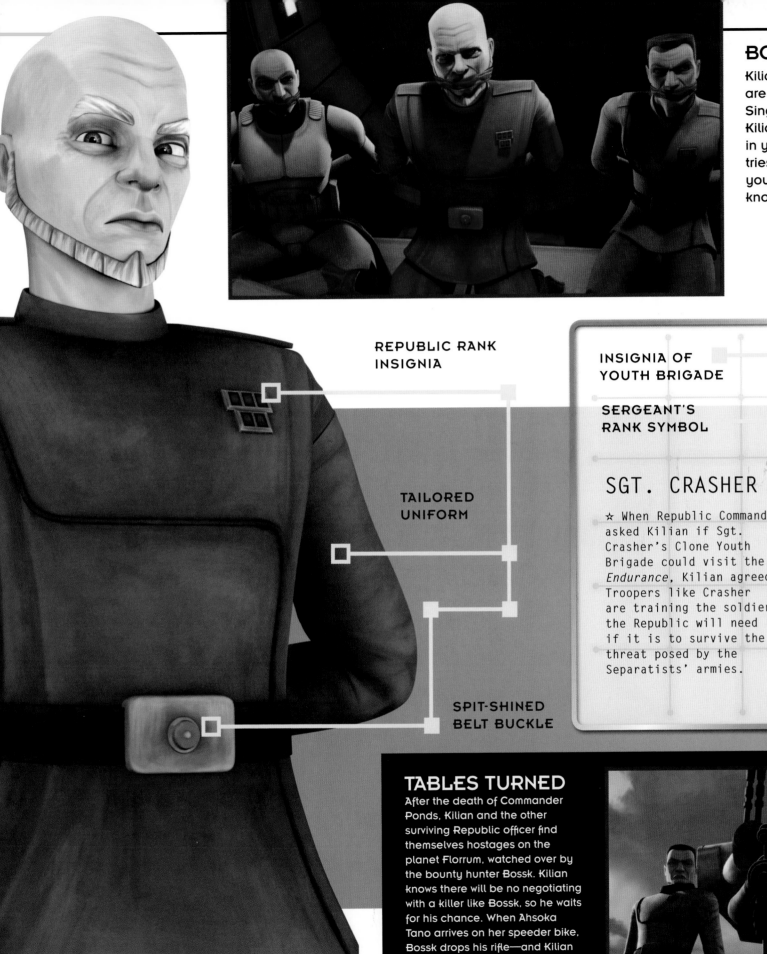

BOBA'S PRISONER

Kilian and two crewmen are taken captive by Aurra Sing's gang of bounty hunters. Kilian sees the uncertainty in young Boba Fett, and tries to help the confused young clone do what he knows is right.

REPUBLIC RANK INSIGNIA

INSIGNIA OF YOUTH BRIGADE

SERGEANT'S RANK SYMBOL

TAILORED UNIFORM

SGT. CRASHER

☆ When Republic Command asked Kilian if Sgt. Crasher's Clone Youth Brigade could visit the *Endurance*, Kilian agreed. Troopers like Crasher are training the soldiers the Republic will need if it is to survive the threat posed by the Separatists' armies.

SPIT-SHINED BELT BUCKLE

TABLES TURNED

After the death of Commander Ponds, Kilian and the other surviving Republic officer find themselves hostages on the planet Florrum, watched over by the bounty hunter Bossk. Kilian knows there will be no negotiating with a killer like Bossk, so he waits for his chance. When Ahsoka Tano arrives on her speeder bike, Bossk drops his rifle—and Kilian sees his opportunity.

AURRA SING

A PALE BOUNTY HUNTER with a cruel smile, Aurra Sing is known as an expert sniper with a blaster rifle, and other hunters fear her ruthlessness. Aurra knew Jango Fett and respected him enough to be a mentor for Boba as he seeks to follow in his father's footsteps and avenge him.

CRACK SHOT
Aurra is rarely seen without her Czerka Adventurer rifle. She is an excellent shot, combining great patience with an eerie calm and remarkably steady hands.

A MYSTERIOUS PAST
Rumors in the galactic underworld say that Aurra was once a Padawan, but either left the Jedi Order or was expelled. Whatever the truth, she hates the Jedi and keeps Padawan braids and lightsabers as grim trophies of victories over them.

VEST MADE OF SHAAK HIDE

NO WITNESS
One lesson Aurra has struggled to teach Boba is that a hunter who commits a crime must never leave any witnesses behind. Hunters must always look out for themselves—pity will only get you into trouble.

BAD COMPANY
Piracy? Kidnapping? Assassinations? It's all the same to Aurra, who doesn't worry about morality as long as she gets paid. Her known associates include the Duros bounty hunter Cad Bane, who hired her to help infiltrate the Senate Building as part of his plan to free the crimelord Ziro the Hutt, as well as the pirate Hondo Ohnaka, a scourge of the Outer Rim.

CZERKA RIFLE AMMUNITION

A HARSH LESSON
Aurra picks up Boba in an escape pod after his ejection from the *Endurance*, and is surprised to find three other clones aboard. Boba wants to let them go, but Aurra is unmoved: The young trainees have seen too much.

LEADER OF THE PACK
Aurra has hired two other bounty hunters to back her up in helping Boba get his revenge against Mace Windu: the Trandoshan hunter Bossk and a Klatooinian named Castas. The Separatists will pay good credits to hunters who eliminate Jedi and bring them Republic officers who can be used as hostages.

ZILLO BEAST

THIS GIGANTIC REPTILE dwells beneath the surface of the planet Malastare, and emerges from a massive crater blasted out by Republic forces. Supreme Chancellor Palpatine takes note of the tough scales that armors the creature, and orders his forces to bring it to Coruscant for a through examination by the Republic's weapons-research department.

SCALES ARE LIGHT BUT VERY TOUGH

DOGE NAKHA URUS

The leader of Malastare's Dugs, Doge Urus knows his planet's great reserves of fuel are critical to the Republic's ability to continue the war, and that Chancellor Palpatine is desperate to secure them for the use of the military. So Urus drives a hard bargain in negotiating a treaty with the Republic. Few Dug leaders ever pass up an advantage!

Sionver Boll

☆ A scientific genius who designed the electro-proton bomb used on Malastare, Dr. Boll is put in charge of discovering if the Zillo Beast has any military value. She wonders if it's right to kill the creature in hopes of aiding the Republic war effort.

DATAPAD HOLDS SCIENTIFIC INFORMATION

BOMBS AWAY

Dr. Boll assures the Jedi that the electro-proton bomb will only damage the Separatists' droids. But the enormous explosive cracks Malastare's surface, creating a giant crater.

TOE PADS HELP BEAST CLIMB WALLS

HORNS USED IN COURTSHIP DISPLAYS

ON THE LOOSE

After the Dugs drive the Zillo Beast out of its crater, Republic tanks try to subdue the giant creature with blasts from their stun cannons.

FORKED TONGUE HELPS SNIFF OUT POTENTIAL MEALS

HARSH DECREE

Malastare's Doge Urus says the Zillo Beast is a bloodthirsty monster, and demands that the Republic help kill it. Palpatine agrees, and ignores Mace Windu's protests that the Beast is innocent and might be the last of its kind.

LIVING FOSSIL

According to Doge Urus, many Zillo Beasts once roamed Malastare, but were killed off when the Dugs began harvesting fuel from the core of the planet. He says an ancient prophecy warned that a Beast would return one day and destroy the Dug civilization.

JEDI VALUES

Mace Windu understands the value of Malastare's fuel to the Republic war effort, but he is appalled by the cruel delight shown by the Dugs as they prepare to kill the Zillo Beast. The creature lived peacefully within Malastare's core, and has only tried to defend itself once disturbed. The Jedi are generals, but Mace decides his duty is to protect an innocent being.

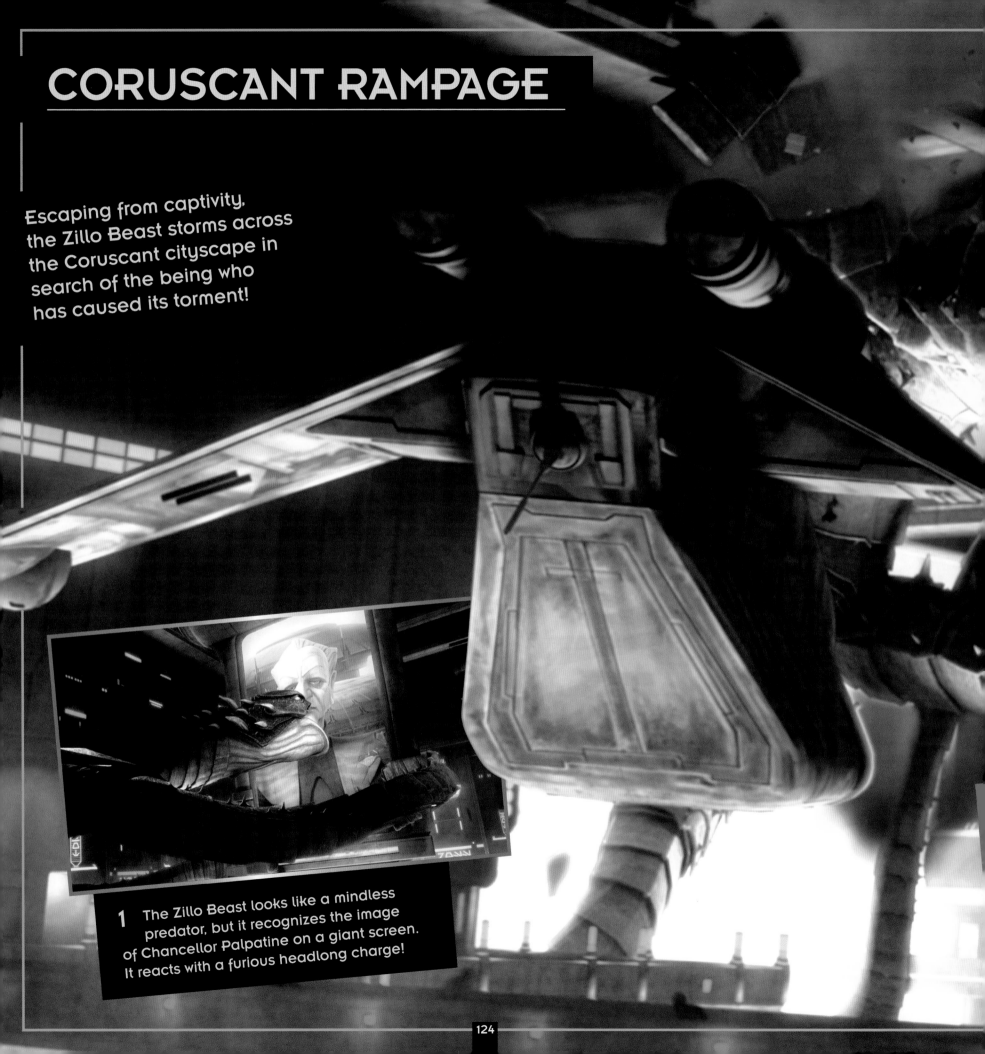

CORUSCANT RAMPAGE

Escaping from captivity, the Zillo Beast storms across the Coruscant cityscape in search of the being who has caused its torment!

1 The Zillo Beast looks like a mindless predator, but it recognizes the image of Chancellor Palpatine on a giant screen. It reacts with a furious headlong charge!

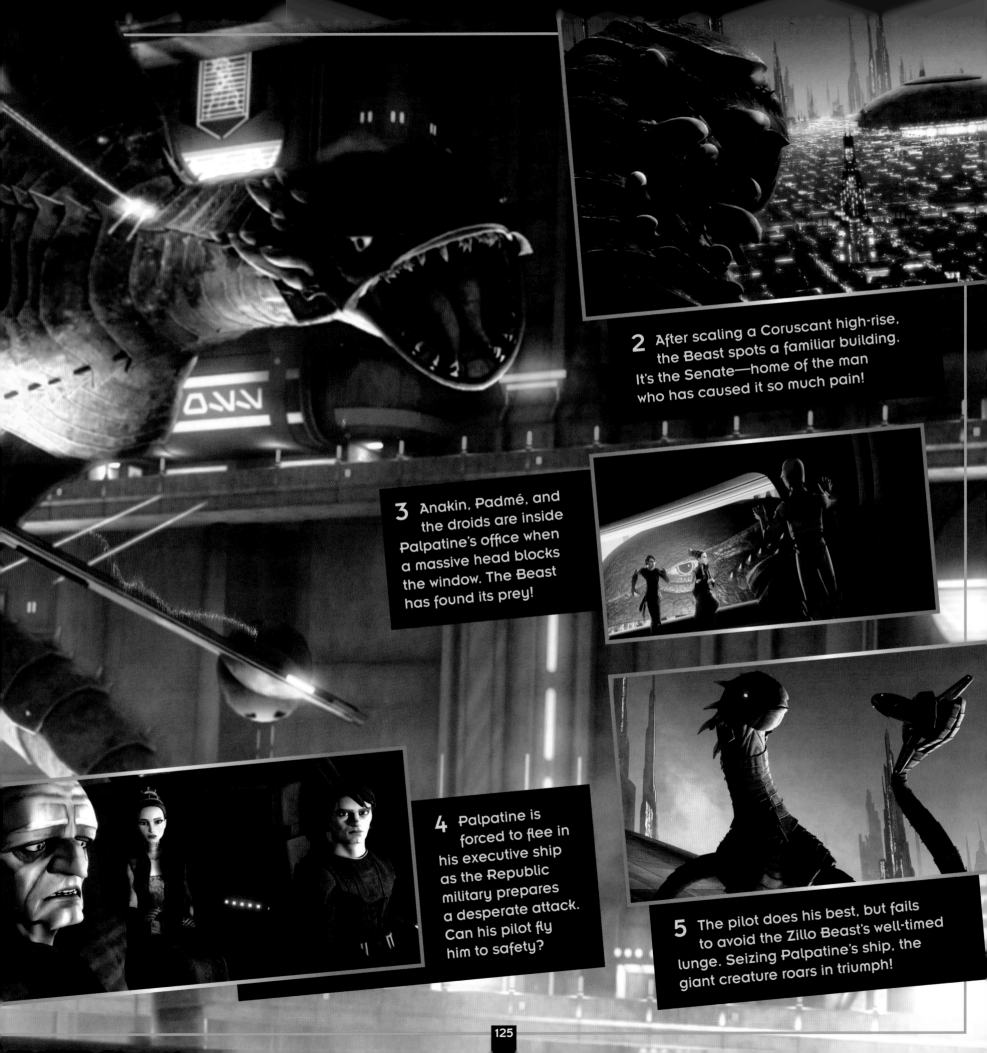

2 After scaling a Coruscant high-rise, the Beast spots a familiar building. It's the Senate—home of the man who has caused it so much pain!

3 Anakin, Padmé, and the droids are inside Palpatine's office when a massive head blocks the window. The Beast has found its prey!

4 Palpatine is forced to flee in his executive ship as the Republic military prepares a desperate attack. Can his pilot fly him to safety?

5 The pilot does his best, but fails to avoid the Zillo Beast's well-timed lunge. Seizing Palpatine's ship, the giant creature roars in triumph!

"THE LINE BETWEEN FRIEND AND FOE IS BLURRED

...NOW MORE THAN EVER."

For Dorling Kindersley

Editor **Victoria Taylor**

Senior Editor **Elizabeth Dowsett**

Designers **Dan Bunyan, Jill Clark**

Senior Designer **Guy Harvey**

Managing Editor **Catherine Saunders**

Art Director **Lisa Lanzarini**

Publishing Manager **Simon Beecroft**

Category Publisher **Alex Allan**

Production Editor **Sean Daly**

Production Controller **Nick Seston**

For Lucasfilm

Executive Editor **J. W. Rinzler**

Art Director **Troy Alders**

Keeper of the Holocron **Leland Chee**

Director of Publishing **Carol Roeder**

First American Edition, 2010

10 11 12 13 14 10 9 8 7 6 5 4 3 2 1

Published in the United States by DK Publishing
375 Hudson Street, New York, New York 10014

177923—06/10
Copyright © 2010 Lucasfilm Ltd and ™.
All rights reserved. Used under authorization.

DK books are available at special discounts when purchased in bulk for
sales promotions, premiums, fund-raising, or educational use.
For details, contact:
DK Publishing Special Markets
375 Hudson Street
New York, New York 10014
SpecialSales@dk.com

A catalog record for this book is available from the Library of Congress.

ISBN: 978-0-7566-6532-6
Color reproduction by MDP
Printed and bound by Leo Paperworks, China

Discover more at
www.dk.com
www.starwars.com